Fir

Approach

Howard Martin

Final Approach

This book is dedicated to my good friend
Dave Norris
who sadly died in an aircraft accident on
Sunday 15th January 2017
R.I.P. Mr Rich

Copyright © 2021 Howard Martin

ISBN-13:9798451904848

Final Approach

Cover image by Fidelity Design
and Print, Unit 7, Kenneth
Way, Wilstead Industrial Park,
Bedford, MK45 3PD, UK,
www.fidelityprint.co.uk
quotes@fidelityprint.co.uk
Tel: +44 (0)1234 907907

CHAPTER ONE

Roger and Alison were eating breakfast.

'Where are you going to live, Roger?'

'What are you on about now, Alison?'

'I'm divorcing you, so I'm asking you where you intend to live?'

'I live here Alison. This is my house. I'm going nowhere. If you want to move out, it's up to you.'

'Well, that's not how I understand the situation, Roger. I'm divorcing you on the grounds of adultery. I think I'll keep the house.'

'Over my dead body.'

'Why don't you rent a flat with Mandy. You can both move in and then you can enjoy as much sex as you both want. You'll probably never even need to turn the heating on.'

'Why don't you just move into Dan's consulting room at the hospital, Alison. You seem to enjoy having sex there, which is more than you do here.'

'Possibly more to do with the person Roger, rather than the venue.'

'Look, I'm sure they purchased Dan's house more with his salary as a gynaecologist at Molden Hospital, rather than Mandy's as a receptionist at the flying club. Surely the sensible thing would be for you two ladies to swap.'

'Whoa, not so fast Roger. Dan lives in Fleawick, I could never live in Fleawick. I was quite happy here until you started flying lessons and cavorting with Mandy. This is your mess, not mine. I don't see why I should lose my home.'

'Unfortunately, I wasn't happy with you Alison. If I hadn't met Mandy, I might have started looking for a position in a monastery.'

'Well, there is your answer, Roger. Either move to a monastery or rent somewhere with Mandy. Looks like you were leaving here anyway.'

Roger kicked himself under the table. He

realised he shouldn't be flippant as Alison was going to take advantage of any weakness. He tried a more serious tack.

'Look, Alison. I bought this house out of what my father left me in his will. I owned it before we got married. I think you'll find that in the eyes of a divorce court, it remains mine.'

'I don't agree, Roger. This is our matrimonial home. You blew our marriage by having sex with Mandy. It's unreasonable to expect me to live with you after that. I want you to go.'

'No way! You did exactly the same with Dan. I want you to go.'

Alison got up. 'But I've got the pictures to prove what you've been up to, Roger. What have you got? Now I'm going to work. Don't be here when I get back!'

Alison went out the front door and slammed it behind her. BANG!

You must be joking, you old harridan thought Roger, *I'm not leaving this house, I purchased it with my legacy.*

CHAPTER TWO

Roger walked into the Flight Training reception. Mandy was behind the desk.

'Hello, Mandy. How are tricks?'

'Dreadful Roger. Dan is adamant he's divorcing me and says he's keeping the house. He suggested I got a flat with you.'

'Then we can have as much sex as we both want. We'll probably never need to turn the heating on?'

'Oh, exactly what he said. How on earth did you know?'

'Because it's what Alison said to me this morning. They obviously have rehearsed it together.'

'He also said he didn't want to find me at home tonight.'

'Alison said the same to me.'

'What are they up to, Roger?'

'Well, it looks like they intend we both end up on the street.'

'While they keep both houses? That wouldn't be fair at all. Yet I've always thought of Dan as a fair-minded person.'

'I don't doubt he still is, but remember he's got Alison pulling his strings now. If he doesn't stand up for himself, she'll wipe the floor with him.'

'He is easily led.'

'I suggested the fairest answer would be for you two ladies to just swap houses.'

'Oh, that sounds lovely, Roger.'

'Unfortunately, Alison says she could never live in Fleawick.'

'Why on earth not?'

'Snobbery really. To be fair, even you refer to it as Lower Linton, rather than Fleawick.'

'True, but only for a laugh. For the most part, it's fine.'

'I don't think we'll ever convince Alison of that. Not that she's got anything to be snobby about. She grew up on the council estate in Molden, and Molden always reminds me of the film Deliverance, minus the banjos. Now, of course, living in such a lovely place as Linton, she'd rather forget her humble beginnings.'

The door to Lewis's office opened and Lewis and Jane emerged. 'Hello, Roger. The weather's not too clever so how about you sit your Navigation and Met exams today? If you pass, we can think about planning your qualifying cross-country.'

'Yes, that's fine Lewis. I've been studying both in my spare time.'

Lewis gave Jane a kiss and she left. 'OK, Roger. Come into my office, and we'll set about it. Mandy, we are not to be disturbed.'

'OK, Lewis.'

CHAPTER THREE

About an hour later, Roger and Lewis came out of Lewis's office.

'Well done, Roger. Next lesson, we'll see about your qualifying cross-country. Keep an eye on the weather and when it looks good, book two slots side by side as it will take up most of a morning or afternoon.' Lewis went back into his office and shut the door.

'I presume you passed OK?' asked Mandy.

'Yes. Both passed, so on to the next challenge. I'd be feeling on top of the world if it wasn't for this divorce business.'

'Yes. It worries me as well. Dan is acting so out of character.'

'Alison is acting so in character. So she'll

be egging him on. Hell knoweth no fury like an Alison scorned. So will you be coming to the bar when you finish?'

'You bet. I'm in need of some TLC.'

Roger looked shocked. 'TLC?'

'Yes, tender loving care.'

'Oh. Good job you explained that. That acronym made me think of something quite different! OK, I'll catch you later.'

Roger left reception and walked across the road to the club bar.

As he walked in, he noticed Kingsley talking to a man at the end of the bar. Judging by the look on Kingsley's face, the conversation didn't appear to be going well. Roger spotted Guy at the other end of the bar and walked over.

'Hello, Guy. What's going on with Kingsley and that chap? Kingsley doesn't look too pleased.'

Guy laughed. 'Oh, that's Phil. He's an engineer for a large car manufacturer and travels a lot in his work, and he keeps offering to bring back menus from the various restaurants he visits on the continent. When he realised that Kingsley didn't like the idea, he did it all the more. He's what we term a wind-up merchant.'

'Well, looks like he's succeeding in winding Kingsley up. His face would stop a tank in its tracks.'

'Yes, Kingsley hates him and refers to him as Mr Menu.'

'So is Enis joining you tonight, Guy?'

'Yes, she should be. Not sure when. She's trying to open her own tattoo parlour in Linton, but she seems to be upsetting the locals somewhat. Lots of opposition. Apparently, a tattoo parlour is not the sort of establishment in keeping with Linton.'

'Why not?'

'Well, I expect the locals are expecting hoards of Hells' Angels on motorbikes flooding the town. But most young people have tattoos these days.'

'Maybe they think using needles will spread aids or something.'

'Good Lord no! Tattoo parlours are so careful to dispose of their needles correctly.'

'Well, Linton residents seem to object to anything new. I expect it will all blow over.'

'You may be right, Roger. Now, tell me, what's this stuff in the bowl they've left out on the bar?'

Roger leaned forward for a better view. 'Er lentils, peanuts, rice, that will be Bombay

Mix.'

'Oh right. I thought they'd hoovered the floor and tipped the dust bag into a dish. Are we supposed to eat it?'

'Yes, it's quite spicy,' said Roger, taking a handful, 'mm, very pleasant.'

'Oh give me a handful of that, I'm starving,' said a voice.

'Oh hello George,' said Roger, and passed the dish to him.

George grabbed a handful and stuffed his mouth full. 'My missus is out with a friend tonight, so no food. I hope Kingsley's menu is in operation.'

'Certainly is, George,' said Kingsley from behind the bar, 'what would you like?'

'Well three pints to start with, and then I'll have a peppered steak please.'

'OK, I'll pull these pints for you, then I'll cook your steak. How would you like it done?'

'Just pull its horns out and wipe its arse, that'll be fine. I'm so hungry I could eat a scabby donkey.'

'Sorry, I won't have those in until next week,' replied Kingsley with a smile as he put three pints on the bar, and scuttled off to his kitchen.

CHAPTER FOUR

'I've passed my Navigation and Met exams today, George.'

'Oh well done, so you'll soon be doing your solo cross-country?'

'Yes, Lewis told me to watch the weather and book a double slot.'

'Well, good luck with that. I think you'll find the cross-country far more enjoyable than even your first solo. Flying over 150 nautical miles and making two full-stop landings at different airfields, getting your paperwork signed up in the tower and starting off again is absolutely magical. If you can do all that, then you've probably got flying cracked.'

'I hope so, George. Flying seems so natural to me now.'

'Once that is out of the way and then there's just a bit of instrument flying to do and your general handling test to pass with an examiner, and bingo, you have a licence.'

'I'm really looking forward to being a pilot, George. Pigs might fly indeed.'

'Pigs might fly?'

'Oh, that was what Alison scrawled on the front of my book when I started my lessons. She obviously didn't think I could do it.'

'Or perhaps she didn't want you to!'

'Possibly. I imagine she had planned to move her mother in and already earmarked the money for the granny flat.'

'I wouldn't want my mother-in-law living with us.'

'Well personally, I wouldn't worry if Alison's mother was pleasant, but she is a right old harridan. No redeeming features at all.'

'Ah, here comes Enis, but she doesn't look too happy,' said Guy, 'Hello Enis, what's the piece of paper in your hand?'

Enis waved the piece of paper in the air, 'Hello Guy, look, those nasty peoples in Linton spread lies about shop. They say there will be needles and blood-stained tissues in the street.'

'Oh no, let me look.' Guy took the piece of paper and started to read. 'This is complete rubbish, Enis. It's libelous. Not complying with environmental health matters, indeed? You had the chap from Environmental Health in the shop this week. He passed everything with flying colours.'

'Yes, he did.'

'So who the hell wrote this rubbish? There is no name on it.'

'No. It is anonymous. Whoever wrote it is liar and coward.'

'Well, I'm not standing for this Enis. We shall fight back. I have a friend who writes articles for the national papers, I'll bring him down to the shop. He may be able to interest ITV as well. This is just pure Linton snobbery.'

'You do all that for me?' Enis threw her arms around Guy, 'Oh Guy, thank you so much, you lovely man.'

'Of course, I will. The accusations they make in this flyer are clearly ridiculous.'

'Well I don't know where Mandy is,' said Roger, 'I thought with the nights drawing in, she'd be finished earlier.'

'Well don't forget pilots start doing their night ratings at this time of year,' said

George, 'it must be dark when you fly or it doesn't count.'

'What do you have to do for a night rating?'

'Basically, five hours flying at night including some more instrument practise, at least three of those must be with an instructor and five solo take-offs and full stop landings.'

'Right, well if I get a licence, a night rating will be the next thing on my list.'

'Well, my offer still stands if you want to fly with me, Roger. I'll help you all I can.'

'Love to George. We must think about the next flight. Where do you fancy?'

'How about a longer flight, somewhere further away?'

'Yes, OK. Where do you suggest?'

'How about Gibraltar?'

'Wow, that is a long way away George, but yes I'm up for it.'

'OK. I'll work out some details, and we'll discuss it another day.'

'Here's your peppered steak, George,' interrupted Kingsley, putting a plate on the bar, 'Three pints and a peppered steak, that's twenty-two pounds please.'

George paid Kingsley and looked around

for somewhere to sit. 'Very busy in here this evening and I don't recognise many faces.'

'They'll be here for my Grab-a-Granny night, George,' said Guy.

'You'd think they'd know better by now,' retorted George as he wandered off to find a spare table.

CHAPTER FIVE

'George is right, the club is filling up nicely now. Word of my grab-a-granny night has spread.'
'If that were true' said Roger, 'surely the place would be empty by now.'
'Ha, bloody ha.'
'I wish you wouldn't keep making jokes about Guy's disco, Roger,' said Enis, 'I told you before, I think disco is very good.'
'It's called banter, Enis. Taking the piss. Humour. Having a laugh. I suppose you do sometimes laugh in Romania or did Ceauşescu put a permanent stop to it?'
'No, he didn't but he tried. Making jokes about him and his awful wife was only thing that kept us going. Now they are dead, I want to dance upon their graves. I lost

several relations to the Securitate.'

'The Securitate?'

'Yes, secret police. They had so many informers on their books that no one say anything against the state. Those that did were arrested, tortured and killed.'

'Well, the first thing that goes in repressive societies is always free speech, as open discussion usually exposes stupidity or corruption. We suffer political correctness here in the UK now, and I expect things will get a lot worse before it gets any better.'

'Ah, but you have democracy. We didn't.'

'Indeed. You didn't need political correctness, because Ceaușescu could kill anyone who disagreed with him. You only need political correctness in a democracy, to wear the population down, to make them conform to some sort of diatribe. Always ends up the same though, a repressive society with no free speech.'

'This conversation is getting heavy,' interrupted Guy, 'Ah here comes George. I hope he enjoyed his steak, oh, maybe not though, he doesn't look too happy.' George walked past them and banged his tray down on the bar.

'What's up, George? Tough steak?'

'The steak was fine.'

'Oh, so what's the matter then? You look really pissed off.'

'I am. I've just seen my next-door neighbour's wife flirting with some low life in the other bar. And it's your grab-a-granny night. God knows what she'll get up to once the music starts.'

Right. No sign of her husband then?'

'No, I know he is working away at the moment. He would be devastated if he knew what she was up to.'

'Well, I think I can only make the situation worse. I do like to use music to get everyone going.'

'I think I need to talk to her, warn her off.'

'Well rather you than me, George,' said Roger, 'Now still no sign of Mandy. I think I'll send her a text, find out how long she'll be.'

'Your phone looks quite modern. Does it have predictive text?'

'Yes. Why do you ask?'

'Because mine has as well and I can't get on with it. When I am away, I like to send my missus a few sexy texts, keep her interested. I sent her one last week when we got stuck in Jersey. So I got home, all expectant like, only to find out that she'd shaved her bloody granny.'

Roger laughed. 'Rule one, always check what you are sending before you actually send it.'

'How was the peppered steak, George?' asked Kingsley from behind the bar.

'Awful, I couldn't eat any of it.'

Kingsley's face fell. 'Oh, I'm sor..,' he looked down at the plate and stopped. The plate was completely empty, not even a trace of the pepper sauce remained. He looked up and saw George was grinning like a Cheshire Cat. Kingsley smiled. 'You bastard, for a moment you had me going there!'

'Absolutely wonderful, Kingsley. I think I'll be eating many more of those.'

'Thank you, George. I'm glad you enjoyed it.'

CHAPTER SIX

'Hello Mandy, I was just going to text you. I wondered where you had got to.'

'Sorry, Roger. The club was very busy tonight with pilots doing their night rating training.'

'Oh right. George thought that might be the trouble. What would you like to drink?'

'I'm gasping. A G and T please.'

Roger caught Kingsley's eye. 'One G and T, three pints, and oh Enis, you haven't had a drink yet. What would you like?'

'Coke, please.'

'And a coke please, Kingsley.'

'So what have I missed?' asked Mandy.

'Oh, nothing much at all. Enis is opening a tattoo parlour in Linton and the locals are up in arms, George found his next-door neighbour's wife cavorting with a low life while her husband is away, Enis wants to dance on the Ceaușescu's graves and George's sex life is being messed up by predictive text. Waste of time you coming in really!'

'So it seems. Another boring night in the Linton Flying Club bar, eh?'

'No, not at all boring,' said Guy, 'remember it's my Grab-a-granny night tonight. Lots of laughs, good music, and dancing.'

Mandy yawned. 'Oh good, you've got a guest DJ on tonight?'

'Ha, bloody-ha.'

Kingsley returned with the drinks. 'There you are, Roger.'

Roger handed him a twenty-pound note. 'Thanks, Kingsley.

'You look different tonight, Guy,' said Mandy, 'and yet I can't work out what it is.'

'Well, I had a haircut today.'

'Oh, that's it! Tell me, why did they completely shave the top off?'

'Another saucer of milk, Mandy? Catty remark or what.'

'Indeed it was Guy. But I only say things like that in the vain hope you might listen to

23

what you say yourself and realise how immature you sound.'

'Well, it's true women do mature a lot earlier than men, Mandy. Women start growing breasts around twelve or thirteen. Men don't start doing that until they're about fifty.'

'Oh I give up,' sighed Mandy, 'I'm going to go, it's been a very long day today.'

Roger, put his pint down on the bar. 'I'll see you to your car, Mandy. Nobody drink that, I'll be back shortly.'

'Just a quick knee-trembler then?' asked Guy.

'Shut up Guy,' said Mandy, 'night all.'

Roger and Mandy left the bar and went into the car park. 'No time for any jollies tonight, Roger. I'm knackered.'

Roger put his arm around her. 'OK, Mandy. Give me a goodnight kiss.'

CHAPTER SEVEN

As Mandy left the car park, a crew bus pulled in and Captain Slack and his crew disembarked. Sandy spotted Roger first.

'Hello, Roger. Going in the club?'

'Yes, Sandy. I've still got a drink in there. Just popped out to say goodnight to Mandy.'

'Oh hello Roger,' said Kyle, 'how's ya belly off for spots?'

Roger held the door to the club open for Sandy. 'About the same as the last time you asked me that, Kyle.'

'Thank you, doorman,' said Kyle and, with another crew member clinging to his arm, followed Sandy into the club.

Roger made a beeline for the bar to retrieve his drink, closely followed by Kyle and the other crew member.

'Roger, I'd like you to meet our newest crew member. Roger, this is Seymour, Seymour Cox. Seymour, this is the Roger I told you about.'

Seymour smiled at Roger and looked him up and down. 'Hello Roger, how bona to vada your dolly old eek.' He turned to Kyle and screwed his face up. 'Nah, he's quite butch, bona lallies and quite a basket on him, and I must admit I wouldn't mind his luppers around me cartso, but he's hardly a dilly boy, is he now?'

Roger looked at Kyle. 'Does he speak any English?'

'Oh that's Polari he's speaking,' explained Kyle.

'Polari? Is he Polish then?'

'Nah, not Polish, it's a language for..'

'Would you like a drink, Roger?' interrupted Sandy.

'Yes please, Sandy. Pint, please. Sorry, Kyle, you were saying?'

'I was saying Polari is a gay language, a sort of code. When it was illegal to be gay, Polari was the only way we could speak to each other without getting arrested.'

'Oh, a bit like cockney rhyming slang,

where you had to be cockney to understand it.

'Yes, I think so. I remember an old radio program called Round The Horne popularised Polari in the sixties.'

'Yes, I've heard some of those episodes on the radio. What were those two called?'

'Oh, that's an easy one,' piped up Seymour, 'Hello, my name's Julian and this is my friend Sandy.'

'Oh, hello Mr Horne!' squawked Kyle.

'Yes every week they were running something different,' said Roger, 'but it was always called Bona whatever. I remember one week they were called Bona Solicitors. Mr Horne wants them to take a case on, but they say they're too busy as they have a criminal practice that takes up most of their time. Mr Horne says that doesn't surprise him.'

'Yes, they were so funny.'

'My father believed that Round The Horne was probably instrumental in the legalising of homosexuality in 1967. Julian and Sandy were loved by millions and the thought of them being persecuted for just being themselves was awful. So their criminal practice was made legal.'

'Oh your Dilly boy is quite the philosopher, isn't he Kyle?'

'Here's your pint Roger,' said Sandy, 'Did I hear my name mentioned?'

'Not unless you were a gay back in the sixties. We were talking about another Sandy.'

'Definitely not me then. I'm strictly hetero. Now I was hoping to catch you tonight Roger, I've got a problem you may be able to help me with.'

'Me? Well, obviously I will if I can. What is it?'

'I need to move some furniture and my flatmate has gone on holiday. I can't move it by myself, and I was wondering if you would help me?'

'Yes, I'm sure I could do that. When do you need it doing?'

'Well, tonight would be good.'

'Methinks the polone can vada his basket and wants his cartso for herself.' squawked Seymour.

CHAPTER EIGHT

Just then Guy started his disco. 'Good
evening, Ladies and gentlemen. Welcome to
the Cloud Nine disco with your host Prince
Charles. Well, what a week it's been. Last
Monday, I went to London and had sex
with a model, which unfortunately led to me
being thrown out of Madame Tussauds. On
Thursday, I made a fool of myself in
Screwfix, well, I wasn't to know. I had
always assumed it was some sort of dating
agency. And then to top it all, yesterday my
girlfriend told me that I was no good in the
bedroom department. But I don't think she
realised how difficult it was for me to
maintain an erection with the department
store manager shouting his bloody head off
at me! Anyway, enough about my troubles,

29

let's start tonight with Trouble by Coldplay from their Parachutes album.'

Roger looked at Sandy. 'Tonight?'

'Yes, well I'll make it worth your while.'

'Oh, isn't she bold?' squawked Seymour.

'I meant, I've some beer in the fridge, Seymour.'

'Well OK, let me finish my pint, and we can go and start moving your stuff.'

'Let's hope the bloody earth moves or there'll be no beer for you, Roger,' said Seymour, with a laugh.

Sandy glared at Seymour. 'Kyle, can you take your friend off somewhere else please before I seriously damage him?'

'OK sister,' said Kyle and dragged Seymour off to the other end of the bar.

'Those two are incorrigible when they are together. Now they're on the same crew, I can't imagine what our passengers must think of them.'

'I would imagine that depends on whether the passengers have a sense of humour or not. I think they're hilarious. Kyle was funny enough on his own but with Seymour with him..,' Roger stopped and burst out laughing. 'Oh, for heaven's sake, Seymour, Seymour Cox, it never hit me when Kyle introduced us. Seymour Cox, is that even his real name?'

'I think so, his name has been on the crew roster.'

'Well, talk about a person having an appropriate name to match their peccadilloes!'

'Yes, indeed err Roger Moore.' Sandy banged her glass down on the bar and grabbed Roger's arm. 'So are you ready to go?'

Roger finished the remaining beer in his glass and smiled at Sandy. 'Yes, I think I..'

Roger's mobile phone interrupted him. He pulled it out of his pocket and looked at the screen. 'Oh, it's Mandy. She went home a while ago. I wonder why she's ringing now?'

'Oh don't answer. I'm sure you'll see her at the club in the morning.'

'No, I'd better answer. She's having problems with her hubby. Hello Mandy, are you alright?'

'No, I'm not, Roger. I can't get into my house. The key doesn't work anymore, so I think Dan has changed the locks.'

'Can't you bang on the door and get him to answer it?'

'No, the house is in complete darkness. I don't think he's at home. What shall I do, Roger?'

'Where are you?'

'Parked outside my house.'

'OK wait there. I'll be straight down.'

Roger put his phone back in his pocket and turned to Sandy. 'I'm terribly sorry Sandy, I'll have to move your furniture some other time. Mandy's in trouble and I really need to help her.'

CHAPTER NINE

Roger left the club, leaving behind a very disgruntled Sandy. He drove from the car park, turned onto the main road, and descended the hill to the ring road, which separated Linton from Fleawick. As he crossed the roundabout, he smiled to himself, recalling how Mandy had referred to the area as Lower Linton, rather than admit she actually lived in Fleawick. He soon spotted Mandy's car and pulled up behind it. He got out and walked round to her driver's door.

'Hello, Mandy, any progress?'

'No, none. The house is still in darkness. He may just be hiding in there but I can't get in.'

'Are there any windows open?'

'Don't think so.'

'Wait here, I'll go and have a look round.'

Roger walked up the path to the front door and looked in. The house did appear to be in darkness. He walked across the lawn and peered in the front window. More darkness. He walked around to the back of the house and looked through the kitchen window. All the windows were shut and the place looked deserted.

Roger noticed a ladder laying up against the fence, so he picked it up and placed it up against the wall underneath the first-floor window, and climbed up. The curtains were closed, so he climbed back down and took the ladder round to the front of the house. A bedroom window above looked slightly open, so he turned to Mandy, who was still sitting in the car, and raised his thumb. Roger put the ladder against the wall and climbed up.

As he got closer to the window, he could see lots of condensation on the inside which wasn't apparent on the other windows. He hauled himself to the top of the ladder and was about to put his arm through the window when a dim light in the room caught his eye. He stopped and stood on tiptoe, so he could look through the small gap in the curtains. Roger gasped. Both Dan and Alison lay on the bed together, stark bollock naked.

Roger's grip on the ladder tightened. His immediate instinct was to open the window, climb in and give Dan a black eye, but he thought back to his conversation with Alison that morning where he had suggested that the best solution was that the girls swapped houses. Roger smiled to himself, climbed down, and replaced the ladder in the back garden where he had found it.

He walked back to Mandy's car. 'OK Mandy, follow me in your car.'

'Where are we going, Roger? I thought you were going to climb in the window and let me in, then you stopped. Why?'

'Dan and Alison are in there, laying stark bollock naked on the bed together. That's fine. Let's do the same round at my house. Follow me.'

Roger got in his car and drove off with Mandy following behind. They crossed the roundabout and climbed the hill back into Linton. Two minutes later they pulled on to Roger's drive.

Mandy got out of her car. 'Oh, what a lovely house, Roger.'

Roger walked to the front door. 'Thanks.'

He put his key in the front door but it wouldn't turn. 'The cow, she's had the locks changed as well. What on earth do those two think it will achieve, locking us both out of our houses? They've lost the plot.'

'What are we going to do now, Roger?'

Roger picked up a small rock from his rockery. 'This,' he said and smashed the small diamond-shaped window in the front door. He put his arm through and opened the door.

'Open sesame,' he said. He picked up Mandy and carried her across the threshold into the house.

'This is a lovely house outside and in,' said Mandy, looking round admiringly.

'Thanks. Can I get you a drink?'

'Yes, a G and T please.'

Roger went to a well-stocked drinks cabinet and poured Mandy a G and T. 'You sit and enjoy your drink, put the TV on if you like. I must fix the front door.'

While Mandy sat and flicked through the channels on the TV, Roger screwed a piece of wood across the broken window. He then removed the lock and replaced it with an old one he found in the garage.

He returned to the front room where Mandy was still happily channel hopping. Roger sat down on the sofa next to her. 'Right, the place is secure again. How are you doing with the TV?'

'I can't believe how many channels you've got. A lot of them are foreign as well and one or two I've flicked through seem to be porn.'

'Well, the continentals are a lot more continental about that sort of thing than we Brits are. I've got a steerable satellite dish, so I can pick up stations from all over Europe. Alison's not interested in the foreign muck as she calls it and prefers Coronation Street.'

'Yes, I think Dan would react to those stations in exactly the same way.'

'Corrie fan, is he?'

'No. He prefers medical soaps, but I suppose that's only to be expected.'

Roger put his arm around her. 'Ready for bed?'

Mandy nodded. 'Oh Roger, I've got nothing with me. No toothbrush, no nightwear.'

'I'll give you a new toothbrush and with

what I have in mind, you most certainly
won't be requiring any nightwear at all!'

CHAPTER TEN

Roger and Mandy were eating breakfast. They both had a smile on their face and were laughing a lot, despite not having had much sleep overnight.

'This is so lovely, Roger,' said Mandy, 'What a wonderful night we had together. Where you got all that energy from, I shall never know.'

'It was the energy I never had a chance to use with Alison, so I sort of stored it up, waiting for the right person to come along.'

'And we're sitting here at breakfast, enjoying each other's company. If I was at home, it would be nothing like this.'

'If it was Alison sitting there instead of you, she would be grumpy and start an argument. Then when I wouldn't give in,

39

she would tell me I was impossible, storm out of the door and slam it behind her.'

'So quite a sea change for us both.'

'Indeed. So are you happy with things as they now are?'

'Of course I am Roger. I spent the night in a fabulous house with a lovely man who has cooked me a wonderful breakfast. What more could a woman ask for?'

'Good. I'm happy with the change too, but as always there is one fly in the ointment, Alison. She won't take this lying down.'

'She was certainly taking it lying down when you peeped through the window last night. '

Roger laughed. 'Yes she was, but that wasn't what I meant. The fact they both changed the locks means they do think they can keep both houses, which is bizarre. When she finds I've changed the lock here, I'm not sure what she will do.'

'On a more practical note though, I've got no clothes. OK, I had a shower but I can't go on like this. What the next move?'

'I'm not sure. Alison hasn't taken anything of hers either. I suppose you could go to Molden hospital and make a scene, you know, wife locked out of her house with no change of clothes. Dan is not going to like that very much, is he?'

Mandy smiled. 'Yes, I could do that. I could really embarrass him.'

'I'm sure you could, but he is not the real problem. As always, Alison is.'

'Couldn't you do the same to her?'

'No, she would soon turn it against me, the unfaithful husband, and she works in a nearly all-women office. Be lucky to get out alive!'

'Yes, I see your point.'

'Tell you what, you go and embarrass Dan and arrange to pick up your clothes at lunchtime. But make sure it is lunchtime, then maybe he won't have time to contact Alison. See if he will give you a key. I'll pack Alison's clothes up, and we'll do a swap. If we get away with it, he'll be a dead man when Alison finds out. She'll go mental.'

'Oh yes, great idea Roger. I'll go straight there before I go to the club. I'll ring Lewis and tell him I'll be a bit late.'

'OK, I'll pack Alison's clothes up, and come into the club. It's going to be a nice day, so I thought I'd plan my solo cross-country this morning and hopefully do it this afternoon. If all goes well, we can pick your clothes up in between.'

'Sounds like a wonderful day, Roger. OK, I'll lay it on thick with Dan, he won't know what hit him!'

Mandy picked her phone up and rang Lewis. 'Hello Lewis, it's Mandy. Look, I've got a bit of a problem to sort out, so I'll be half an hour late in. Can you hold the fort? OK thanks, see you soon.'

'Was he OK?'

'Oh Lord yes, the extra time I put in at the club and don't get paid for, half an hour is nothing.'

Roger put his arm around her and gave her a kiss. 'OK, good luck with Dan. I'll see you soon.'

Mandy picked her handbag up and went to the door. 'See you.' She left and closed the door quietly behind her.

Wow! thought Roger, *the door must be wondering why it wasn't slammed.*

CHAPTER ELEVEN

Roger walked into the Flight Training reception. Mandy was behind the counter and looked quite pleased with herself.

'How did it go, Mandy?'

Mandy smiled and held up a key. 'Like a dream, Roger. He couldn't get rid of me fast enough. I felt quite sorry for him really because he's not at all nasty.'

'No, I'm sure it's all Alison's doing and you did say he was easily led.'

'Yes, he is. Anyway, I've got the new key. He said to pop it back through the letterbox when I'd finished.'

'Well I've got Alison's clothes and toiletries packed in the car, so we can do a swap at lunchtime. Now I need to plan my qualifying cross-country, is Lewis in his

43

office?'

'Yes, just knock on the door.'

Roger knocked then opened the door. On the other side, Lewis and Jane sprang apart like two similar poles on magnets. 'Sorry, Lewis. I need to plan my solo cross-country, so could you brief me as to where I'm going?'

'Yes, of course, Roger. Go into the briefing area, and I'll join you in a minute and show you on a map.'

Roger left Lewis's office and went into the briefing area. Lewis eventually joined him.

'The standard route for a solo cross-country from Linton is Linton to Coventry, Coventry to Leicester, and Leicester back to Linton. That meets all the CAA requirements and the airfields are used to seeing our aircraft, so they will sign all the paperwork without any hassle.'

'You need to take the paperwork up to the tower and ask the ATC chappie to sign to say that you were alone in the aircraft. OK, so draw the tracks on your map, work out the times and headings using the met information, and don't forget to check NOTAMs. You don't want to mix with a Royal Flight or an air show. When you have finished, bring the plan to my office for checking.'

'OK Lewis, thanks. I'll see you with the completed flight plan.'

Roger got out his map and marked the required tracks between the three airports with his chinagraph pencil. He measured the bearings of the tracks and copied them to his flight plan. Then he applied the forecast two thousand foot wind to each one to work out the heading he would have to hold and the ground speed he would achieve.

He measured the distance between each airport and now knowing the ground speed he worked out the flight time on each leg. He marked a few ground features on each leg to check his progress and noted all the radio frequencies he would need to call, both en-route and destination. Finally, he checked NOTAMs for any Royal flights or other events that could cause him problems. After about half an hour, he felt confident in what he had achieved and took it all to Lewis's office. 'Here you are Lewis, I think this is all correct.'

'OK Roger, leave it on my desk and I'll look at it in a minute.'

Roger deposited the map and paperwork on Lewis's desk. 'Is it OK to take Mandy for an early lunch, we've got some errands to run?'

'Yes, that's OK, Roger. We're not busy.'

Roger went back out into reception. 'Come on Mandy, it's time to do the great swap.'

CHAPTER TWELVE

Roger and Mandy left the club and
jumped into Roger's car.

Mandy looked round to the back seats.
'Heavens, what a load of stuff Alison has.'

Roger laughed. 'The boot is full to the
brim as well.'

They drove from the car park onto the
main road, down the hill into Fleawick, and
pulled up outside Mandy's house.

'You go and start collecting your stuff
together while I bring Alison's stuff indoors,
then we can repack these cases and boxes
with your stuff.'

Mandy opened the front door and rushed
upstairs while Roger struggled up the path
with lots of cases and boxes.

He put them down in the hall and began

to unpack as Mandy descended the stairs with armfuls of her clothes.

'Here, start to fill these as I empty them.'

Mandy dumped the clothes into an empty suitcase and ran upstairs again.

Working together, it wasn't very long before the exchange was complete.

'OK Mandy, let's put these cases back into the car.'

They carried some suitcases down to the car and went back for the boxes.

'Right we're all loaded,' said Roger, 'let's go home and unload.'

'OK,' said Mandy, 'I'll go and lock up and drop the key through the letterbox.'

Mandy went back to the house and locked the door. She dropped the key through the letterbox.

She climbed back into the car. 'All done.'

'You should have kept the key in case you've forgotten anything.'

'No, I couldn't possibly do that, Roger. That wasn't what I agreed with Dan.'

'Yes you're right, he's in enough trouble already. What sort of flowers does he like?'

'Flowers? I'm not sure, why do you ask?'

'Well as I told you this morning, he'll be a dead man when Alison finds out what has happened. I'd like to give him a good funeral.'

Mandy looked shocked. 'Surely you're not serious Roger. She wouldn't do that, would she?'

'No. Just a little light torture perhaps, pull out a couple of his toenails or wire his testicles up to the mains. But seriously, I think he'll see Alison as she really is for the first time.'

Roger started the car, and they drove back out of Fleawick and up into Linton. They pulled onto Roger's drive.

'OK let's dump these cases and boxes inside the house and sort them out when we are at home this evening. I need to move on my qualifying cross-country.'

Roger went and opened the front door while Mandy started bringing some boxes in. Roger collected the suitcases and in a couple of minutes, they were on the road again back to the club.

As they walked back into the club reception, Lewis was sitting at Mandy's desk and on the phone.

'Yes, yes, I do understand but oh hang on, here he is now.' Lewis put his hand over the mouthpiece, 'It's your wife Roger, apparently, she can't get into your house. This is the second time she's called, and she seems pretty upset.'

He handed Roger the phone. 'Yes, Alison?'

'I can't get in the house, Roger.'

'Funny that Alison, I had similar problems yesterday.'

'So you've changed the locks?'

'Yes, I did. You gave me the idea.'

'But I need to get in.'

'No, you don't need to. I've dropped all your things down at Dan's place.'

'At Dan's place? When?'

'When I picked up Mandy's stuff about half an hour ago.'

'But how.., was Dan there?'

'No.'

'So how did you get in?'

'Dan gave Mandy a key.'

'He did what?'

'Sounds the sensible option all-round, Alison. He's got who he wants to live with him, I've got who I want living with me and Mandy is living with who she wants. But I suppose you are going to be the fly in the bloody ointment as always.'

'You bet I am Roger. My solicitor will

have you out of that house in no time. I'm
not taking this lying down.'

'You were taking it lying down last night.'

'What?'

'Well, Mandy couldn't get in her house
last night. I was trying to help her by
climbing in a window. Luckily, I had a peek
through the curtains of the front bedroom
before I climbed in and that's when I saw
you taking it lying down.'

Click. The line went dead. Roger put the
phone down.

'She hung up. Typical, when she's losing
an argument.' Roger turned to Lewis, 'Now
did you check my flight plan?'

'Yes, Roger. Here it is. It looks fine. But
are you sure you want to do it today?'

'Why on earth not?'

'You've just had a blazing argument with
your wife. Are you sure you're in the right
frame of mind? A qualifying cross-country
takes a lot of concentration.'

'Yes, I'm sure.'

'Well, I suggest you leave as soon as
possible as the nights are really drawing in
now. If you hit any problems ring me, I
can't have you flying about in the dark.'

'Will do. Mandy, can you book me out in

Hotel Tango, please? OK I'll see you both later.'

'Wait, don't forget this form, Roger. You must ask Air Traffic to sign and stamp it as proof you actually arrived and there was no one with you.'

Roger took the form and left the building.

'What was that all about with his wife?' asked Lewis.

'Probably best you don't know,' said Mandy.

CHAPTER THIRTEEN

Roger walked over to Hotel Tango and took his flight plan, map and checklist from his case, and placed them on the pilot's seat, carefully stowing his case into the rear of the aircraft.

He picked up the checklist and walked around the aircraft making sure it was structurally sound. He checked the oil, visually checked the contents of the fuel tanks, and finally climbed into the aircraft and shut the door.

'Clear prop,' he shouted and started the engine, making sure the oil pressure rose into the green on the gauge.

'Linton Tower, Hotel-Tango request taxi for flight to Coventry.'

'Roger, Hotel-Tango. PTT switch

Malcolm here. Good luck on your qualifying cross-country, Roger. Clear taxi to the holding point for runway two-six. QNH One-zero-one-four.'

'Thanks, Malcolm, clear taxi to the holding point two-six, One-zero-one-four.'

Roger released the brakes and taxied towards the holding point. He tried to concentrate on the task at hand but his mind kept thinking back to what Alison had said about her solicitor.

On reaching the holding point, Roger stopped the aircraft, opened the checklist, and started to run through a long list of checks. He knocked his hand on the control column and dropped the checklist. Roger retrieved it from the floor, but he had lost his place. He thought he remembered where he got to and continued to the end of the list.

'Linton Tower, Hotel-Tango ready for departure.'

'Roger Hotel-Tango. Cleared take-off runway two-six. QNH One-zero-one-four.'

'Cleared take-off runway two-six. QNH One-zero-one-four.'

Roger released the brakes and taxied onto the runway. He opened the throttle, accelerated down the runway, and took off.

He climbed to five hundred feet and started a climbing turn to bring him back into the overhead at two thousand feet, so he could start the first leg of his journey.

Roger looked at the direction indicator, turned onto his outbound heading and started his timing. Down in the tower, Malcolm looked puzzled. He looked at where the aircraft was heading and tried to reconcile it with where Roger had said his destination was.

'Hotel-Tango, confirm your destination is Coventry?'

Roger was surprised. 'Confirm Coventry,' he said.

'Are you sure you are on the right heading?'

Roger looked down at his flight plan, checked the heading, and then looked at the direction indicator. Yes, they matched, so what was Malcolm on about? He looked up at the magnetic compass in the windscreen and spotted the problem immediately. A thirty-degree discrepancy.

Then it hit him, when he dropped the checklist he had missed out on the check of aligning the direction indicator with the compass. He held the aircraft steady and twisted the knob on the direction indicator to align the two.

'Thanks, Malcolm,' he said sheepishly, 'schoolboy error on my part! I think I owe you a pint or two.'

'No problem,' said Malcolm, 'that's what we are here for. Hotel-Tango cleared to en-route frequency.'

'Cleared to en-route frequency. Hotel-Tango.'

Roger tried to put Alison out of his mind and concentrate on the flight. He looked down at his flight plan for his first ground feature. It was Molden Hospital again, which Roger spotted off his starboard wing. He turned the aircraft and flew in that direction, turning on to his correct heading when he reached it. Molden bloody hospital, he thought and his mind turned back to think about Alison and Dan in Dan's consulting room.

CHAPTER FOURTEEN

The flight progressed, and each way-point came and went more or less on time. Roger felt pleased. So pleased he didn't notice the cloud-base lowering and the amount of cloud increasing until suddenly he went totally into cloud.

Roger was taken aback. The met report had forecast good conditions, a four thousand feet cloud base with only a ten per cent chance of a shower. He looked down at his flight plan. What was his safety altitude for this leg? One thousand five hundred feet. Roger pushed forward on the control column and hoped he came out the bottom of the cloud above that height and the right way up!

After a few seconds, he emerged from the

bottom of the cloud in a slight left turn. He straightened the wings and checked his heading. He had just started to turn back on track when the sky went black and the rain hit. The noise was deafening. Rivulets of rain ran down the windshield and the aircraft started to buffet. Luckily Roger recalled his recent experience on the way back from Jersey, and he knew there was no need to panic. He looked out the side window and saw he was above an industrial estate. He decided to fly in a circle around the factories until the rain stopped, rather than to fly on aimlessly and risk getting lost. After the third circuit, the noise of the rain increased and hailstones began to hit the aircraft. Roger crossed his fingers and hoped one wouldn't smash the windshield. Then, as suddenly as it had started, the rain stopped and the sky brightened.

As the sun came out again, Roger turned to regain his track and climbed back to his cruising altitude. He spotted his next way-point in the distance and started to fly towards it. As he neared it, he could see Coventry Airport in the distance, basking in the sunshine. He checked the frequency displayed on the radio against his flight

plan. 'Coventry Information, good
afternoon, Hotel-Tango inbound to you
from Linton.'

'Hotel Tango, good afternoon, join left-
base for runway two-three, QFE one-zero-
zero-two. Wind three-two-zero at ten knots.
You are number one.'

'Join left-base for runway two-three, QFE
one-zero-zero-two. Hotel-Tango.'

Roger set the QFE on the altimeter,
reduced power, and turned the aircraft
towards left base. He kept the aircraft
descending and turned on to finals at eight
hundred feet.

'Hotel-Tango, finals.'

'Roger, Hotel-Tango. Clear to land, wind
three-one-zero at twelve knots.'

'Clear to land, Hotel-Tango.'

Unfortunately, as he turned on to final
approach, he forgot to allow for the
crosswind and soon found himself drifting
left of the centre line. He stepped hard on
the right rudder and swung the aircraft's
nose into the wind. He held it until he
regained his position and then adjusted the
yaw as the wind reduced during his descent.
As he came over the threshold, he kicked
the aircraft straight with the left rudder and

gently lowered it onto the tarmac.

'Hotel-Tango, we are expecting you, so park in front of the tower and bring your paperwork up for signature.'

Roger taxied over to the front of the tower and parked. He got out and took the paperwork up the stairs into the tower.

'Hello, you must be Roger,' said the controller, 'PTT switch Malcolm phoned and told me to expect you. You're a bit late but I expect you met that heavy shower on the way.'

'Yes I did,' replied Roger, 'Err did Malcolm tell you why he's called PTT switch Malcolm?'

The controller looked embarrassed. 'Er yes, he did. But I sort of knew already as I think we've got quite a few copies of that recording circulating around in our flying club.'

'Bloody hell, wherever I fly, that incident will always follow me around.'

'Well, I wouldn't worry about it, Roger. Pity you can't stay. I'm sure all the guys in the flying club would love to buy you a pint, just to say they've had a drink with the man on the recording. Now, let me sign your paperwork and you can get on your way.'

Roger handed him the paperwork, and he hastily filled it in and handed it back.

'Well nice to have met you, Roger. I'm Richard by the way. I'll let Leicester know to expect you once you're airborne, I'm sure they'll be pleased to meet the man on the recording as well!'

Roger went back down the stairs and climbed into the aircraft. He sat for a moment and wondered where else that recording had got to. Would he one day land in Australia, only to be confronted with 'Hello Roger old sport, does it look like a jewel in a velvet case or a nasty road accident today?'

He started the engine. 'Hotel-Tango, request taxi for Leicester.'

'Hotel-Tango cleared to taxi to the holding point runway two-three. QNH one-zero-one-one.'

'Cleared taxi to the holding point runway two-three. QNH one-zero-one-one. Hotel-Tango.'

Roger increased the engine power and taxied around the perimeter of the airfield to the runway. He completed his final checks. 'Hotel-Tango, ready for departure.'

'Hotel-Tango cleared take-off runway

two-three. Wind three-one-zero at eight knots.'

'Cleared take-off runway two-three, Hotel-Tango.'

CHAPTER FIFTEEN

Roger opened the throttle and Hotel-Tango sped down the runway. At 65Kts he pulled back on the control column and Hotel-Tango leapt into the air. At five hundred feet, Roger began a climbing turn on track for Leicester. He levelled off at fifteen hundred feet.

'Hotel-Tango, give Leicester a call now on one-two-two-decimal-one-two-five. They're expecting you. Good luck.'

'One-two-two-decimal-one-two-five. Thanks, Richard.'

Roger changed the frequency on the radio. 'Leicester, good afternoon, Hotel-Tango.'

'Good afternoon, Hotel-Tango. Runway two-eight in use, QFE is niner-niner-seven.

Report field in sight.'

'Runway two-eight, niner-niner-seven, Hotel-Tango.'

Leicester is only twenty-two nautical miles from Coventry and already the town stood out quite clearly. As he crossed the M1 motorway, he spotted the airfield to the southeast of Leicester.

'Hotel-Tango, field in sight.'

'Roger Hotel-Tango. Clear land runway two-eight. Surface wind three-one-zero at eight knots.'

'Clear land runway two-eight, Hotel-Tango.'

Roger was surprised to receive landing clearance so far out and concluded that the airfield couldn't be busy. Five minutes later, he landed on the numbers and looked around for the tower. He spotted a glass-fronted building with a glass observation deck on top and taxied towards it.

He was surprised at the number of people that were standing outside. Roger brought the aircraft to a stop on the grass in front, shut the engine down, and jumped out. He was greeted with a cheer from the crowd, and then he heard his voice coming in unison from several mobile phones, '.. a

jewel in a velvet case .. nasty road accident..'.
Roger was stunned.

As he made his way through the crowd,
people slapped him on the back and said
'Good luck, Roger!' He climbed the steps
and went up into the tower.

'Hello Roger, I'm Brian. Did you enjoy
the reception?'

'Yes, My flabber has never been quite so
ghasted.'

'Well that recording is quite popular in the
club so when we heard the perpetrator was
coming, everyone wanted to meet you. The
circuit is empty, the bar is empty, actually,
you are costing the club a small fortune.'

'I'm sorry about that. If I had known I
was so popular, I'd have brought some
signed photographs to sell.'

'Well in the interests of the club remaining
solvent, the faster I sign your piece of paper,
the faster normality will return.'

Roger handed Brian his paperwork. Brian
signed it and handed it back. 'Well nice to
meet you, Roger. I'll let Linton know you're
on your way back as soon as you're
airborne. In fact, you need to get your skates
on if you are going to make it back before
dark.'

'Thanks, Brian.' Roger shook Brian's outstretched hand and left the tower. He went back down the stairs to the still assembled welcoming committee. A rather pretty girl grabbed his arm. 'Hello Roger, I'm Julie. Do fly back sometime and stay for a drink. Stay overnight if you like, I can guarantee you a bed.'

'Thanks, Julie, I'll remember that but I have to be off now, so I can get back to Linton before dark.'

Roger made his way through the crowd and walked to the aircraft. He stopped and waved to the crowd before he got in. He started the engine. 'Leicester, Hotel-Tango requesting taxi for flight back to Linton.'

'Roger Hotel-Tango. The airfield is all yours. Cleared taxi to and take-off from runway two-eight. QNH one-zero-one-one.'

'Cleared take-off runway two-eight. QNH one-zero-one-one.'

Roger taxied to the holding point and completed his checks. He taxied onto the runway, opened the throttle, and soon became airborne. He looked down at the club and noticed the crowd had disappeared apart from one person still waving madly. Roger screwed his eyes up trying to see who. He smiled to himself. The very pretty Julie.

The rest of the flight was uneventful, although Roger was concerned at the failing light. He hadn't landed in the dark before, and he didn't want to prang the aircraft. In the failing light, Roger could just make out the town of Linton ahead, with Fleawick to the south and Molden to the east.

'Linton Tower, Hotel-Tango inbound to you from Leicester.'

'Roger, Hotel-Tango. Cleared land runway two-six. QFE niner-niner six.'

'Cleared land two-six. QFE niner-niner six. Hotel-Tango.'

As Roger turned onto final approach, he noticed the runway was not only lined on both sides with lights which made it easy to see, but also the approach to the runway itself was clearly marked out with red and white approach lights.

He turned Hotel-Tango's landing light on which lit the runway up as he came in over the threshold. He landed without incident and taxied back to the club.

I can't wait to start my night rating he thought.

CHAPTER SIXTEEN

Roger walked back into the Flight Training reception area. Lewis and Mandy were waiting for him.

'Oh Roger, I'm so pleased you are back. We were starting to worry,' said Mandy.

'How did it go Roger?' asked Lewis, 'Is everything signed, any problems?'

'Well I ran into a heavy shower on the way to Coventry and it slowed me down a bit, but otherwise no problems.' Roger handed Lewis the paperwork, 'Everything is signed off I think.'

Lewis ran his eye over the paperwork. 'Yes, looks fine Roger. So just some instrument flying to do and then your GFT.'

'My GFT?'

'Your general flying test, with an

examiner. I can do the instrument flying training with you but I can't do the GFT. I know a chap called Dave Norris who is an examiner, I'll ask him to do it for you.'

'OK, so when can we do that?'

'Well we can do the instrument training next lesson but I need to ask Dave when he's available. He's a Garage Magnate.'

'A Garage Magnate? Is that anything like a fridge magnet?'

'No, not unless you make a fortune from selling fridges. Dave owns a chain of garages in various towns. He's mega-rich, he only became an instructor and examiner because he loves flying.'

'OK, so we'll do the instrument flying tomorrow if we can, and if you can contact Dave please, to find out when he's available.'

'Will do,' said Lewis and disappeared back into his office.

Roger put his arm around Mandy. 'I think I'll go into the club for a drink now. I'll see you when you finish.'

'You bet.'

Roger left and walked over the road into the club bar. Straight away he noticed Kingsley in conversation again with wind up merchant Phil. Phil had what looked like menus in his hand and again Kingsley had a face as black as thunder.

Roger went to the bar close enough to overhear their conversation.

'I could very easily cook all the dishes on the menu from the Hotel Plaza Athena in Paris, Philip. Alaine Ducasse is a personal friend, but they are not appropriate for a small flying club.'

'But I think they would go down a treat in here, Kingsley, compared to what you are offering.'

'My home-made pies are extremely popular in here, Philip. George loves my peppered steak, and snacks like cheesy French fries and burgers are my best-sellers.'

Roger decided to rescue Kingsley. 'Kingsley, pint please.'

'Sorry, Roger, of course.' Kingsley moved up the bar at speed, grabbed a glass, and began pouring a pint.

Kingsley put the pint on the bar. 'Here, that pint is on me. Keep talking, so I don't need to go back to Phil.'

'He's still driving you up the wall is he?'

'Oh, you know about that do you?'

'Yes, Guy filled me in on the subject. You

know he's deliberately winding you up, don't you?'

'He's certainly is. It's hellish.'

'Oh ignore him. If you don't bite, he can't do it. So where's Fidel tonight?'

'He's out looking at a car he wants us to buy.'

'Let me guess what type. A Daimler or a Jaguar?'

'Lord no, we couldn't afford either. No, Fidel has always wanted a Smart Car.'

'One of those little two-door jobs?'

'Yes. If we buy it, he's going to have to learn to drive. I'm fed up with doing all the driving. Anyway, how's your flying going?'

'Fine thanks. I completed my solo cross-country this afternoon.'

'I've no idea what you are on about but it sounds as if congratulations are in order.'

'It means I'm nearing the end of the course now. Not much to do before I get my licence.'

'Oh that's brilliant,' said a voice, and Roger turned round to find George and Guy had walked in.

'Hello George, hello Guy. Yes, solo cross-country finished and signed up. Can I buy you both a drink? I'm celebrating.'

'That sounds like two pints to me.'

'A pint for George and Guy please Kingsley, and something for yourself.'

'So you've still got some instrument flying left to do I think.'

'Yes, hopefully, we are going to do it tomorrow. What does it entail?'

'Using the artificial horizon instead of the horizon you see out the window. Also, you can get secondary information from other instruments such as the altimeter, airspeed indicator, and the turn and slip. It's all a matter of hand-eye coordination training.'

'I use Baywatch for my hand-eye coordination training,' said Guy, 'darn sight cheaper than learning to fly.'

'I would have thought Enis would have weaned you off that by now.'

'So just your GFT left to do, who is going to do that for you?'

'A chap called Dave Norris according to Lewis.'

George smiled. 'Oh, Mr. Rich. Brilliant. He's a lovely chap, and he'll give you a fair test. Now, Kingsley, I'm in urgent need of one of your wonderful peppered steaks.'

'It'll be with you in a jiffy,' said Kingsley and rushed off to his kitchen.

CHAPTER SEVENTEEN

'Have you thought any more about our next flight, George?' asked Roger.

'Well as I said the other night, I thought perhaps a longer sortie. I mentioned Gibraltar then, but how about Malta?'

'Well they are both brilliant destinations, but how long a trip are we talking about?'

'Well perhaps Malta is a bit far for this time of the year so let's concentrate on Gibraltar. Basically, an eight-hour trip, stopping off at Biarritz to refuel. So two four-hour legs. How long we stop in Gibraltar is another matter. Shame to go all that way and not see the sights.'

'Indeed but both Mandy and I have domestic problems at the moment and I wouldn't want to be away for more than a couple of days.'

'OK, what about passengers? Me, you and Mandy, Guy, are you and Enis up for it?'

'Well I certainly am, but I don't think Enis will be as she has just opened her tattoo parlour.'

'OK, so we need two more people, any ideas?'

'I'll ask Mandy,' said Roger, spotting Mandy coming through the door.

'Your steak is ready George,' shouted Kingsley from behind the bar.

'OK guys, I'm off to eat, see what you can sort out.'

'What did George want us to sort out?'

'We've been talking about a trip to Gibraltar, but we're a couple of people short. Can you think of anyone else who might like to join us?'

'No. Most people I know think light aircraft are death traps and can't understand why I do the job I do.'

'OK, well never mind, I'm sure we'll find someone. Now, Mandy, I'm absolutely knackered after my solo cross-country, do you mind if we go? There's plenty of G and T at home.'

'Of course not.'

'Oh don't go,' said Guy, 'Stay for my disco, that'll liven you up.'

'No thanks, Guy. Must rush, I need to pull a couple of fingernails out when I get home.'

'OK, but don't forget to come down to the tattoo parlour tomorrow, see Charlie Garth or maybe ITV interview Enis.'

'Oh, does Charlie Garth look like a pig and wear a grey trilby hat with a ticket in the band marked press?' asked Mandy.

'I'm sure he doesn't look like a pig but yes I think he wears a grey trilby hat but I've never noticed a ticket with press written on it. Where did you get all that from?'

'Spitting Image on TV. Don't you remember all the reporters looked like that?'

'Oh yes, now you mention it, I do. Well, you can decide if he fits that description tomorrow.'

'OK, we will be there.'

Roger and Mandy walked towards the door as Captain Slack and his crew walked in with Kyle and Seymour leading the way. Seymour spotted Roger.

'Oh look Kyle, it's your Dilly Boy with a polone.'

'Hello Roger, how bona to vada your dolly old eek.'

'Well, that makes a change from your usual greeting Kyle.'

'I'm teaching him all the Polari,' said Seymour.

'Wonderful,' said Roger and opened the door, only to find Sandy there. He stepped to one side to let her into the bar. 'Hello, Sandy.'

Sandy looked at him with a stony face and walked right past him and Mandy without speaking.

'What's the matter with her,' asked Mandy.

'No idea. Oh, hold on though, she wanted me to help her the other night. We were just off as you rang to say you were locked out. Perhaps that's what it is.'

'So what did she want you to do?'

'Move some furniture in her flat. Her flatmate was away, and she needed it done that night.'

'You idiot. She was after your body and you let her down, right at the last minute. Probably cost her a small fortune in batteries! That's what's upset her.'

CHAPTER EIGHTEEN

Roger and Mandy were enjoying breakfast.

'Thank you for another exhausting night, Roger. But I need some sleep!'

'Well, you weren't so bad yourself. Is your fry up alright?'

'Lovely thanks, I never got this at home. I was always doing the cooking.'

'Well, I only cook because Alison was too bloody lazy. Otherwise, I'd have gone hungry.'

'Probably the same reason I did it.'

'Are you coming down to the tattoo parlour this morning? Be interesting to watch Enis's interview and also to meet Charlie Garth.'

'Oh yes, I wouldn't miss it. I told Lewis

that I would be late in today. He said fine, as the weather forecast wasn't up to much, so he would be stuck in the office.'

'Good. Should be fun. Oh, here's the postman.'

Roger got up, walked to the front door, and picked up the post. He looked at one of the envelopes and his brow furrowed. 'It's from a solicitor.'

Roger sat down and opened the envelope. He took the letter out and started reading. His brow furrowed further and his jaw dropped. 'The cheeky cow!'

'Bad news?'

'Yes, from Alison's solicitor. She's divorcing me on the grounds of adultery, and she says I've locked her out of her own home and installed my concubine. She wants possession of the house and us to leave forthwith. Typical Alison, no mention of the fact that she's committed adultery and locked me out of my home as well!'

'What are you going to do, Roger?'

'I'm going to ignore it but also go to a solicitor myself. Find out what the legal position actually is.'

'Good idea.'

'I'm not giving up without a bloody fight.

I've never been as happy as I am now.'

'Oh Roger.' Mandy lent over and gave Roger a kiss.

'Have you heard anything from Dan?'

'No, not a thing.'

'Could mean either he is happy living with Alison or maybe she has killed him after all.'

'Don't exaggerate Roger.'

'OK, well perhaps she's tied him to a chair naked and is periodically connecting his testicles to the mains.'

'Did she do that to you then?'

'No, but I stand up to her. Show any sign of weakness and you're finished.'

'Well while I can't say Dan is assertive, he is a professional and I can't believe he would let himself be treated badly.'

'Professional yes, I mean he is just the person you would want around if you were pregnant. Mind you, he would also be pretty useful in a power cut.'

'In a power cut?'

'Yes, that light on his forehead could prove invaluable.'

Mandy laughed and shook her head. 'Come on, we'd better go, or we'll miss Enis's interview.'

CHAPTER NINETEEN

Roger and Mandy walked into Enis's tattoo parlour. There was quite a bit of activity, lots of people and a TV camera. Roger spotted Enis and Guy at the back of the shop, deep in conversation with a couple of people, so they went over.

'Hello Enis, Guy. Well, what a turnout. You must be really pleased.'

'Oh Roger, Mandy, thank you so much for coming. Yes, is good. Thanks to Charlie, we have ITV here as well..'

Guy interrupted her. 'Roger, Mandy, can I introduce Charlie Garth. Charlie, this is Roger, he's learning to fly at the Linton Flying Club and this is Mandy, who is the club's receptionist.'

'Pleased to meet you,' said Charlie with a

big smile, slipping his arm around Mandy's waist. 'Are all the girls at the flying club as pretty?'

'No, she's definitely the prettiest,' said Roger, 'I'm a lucky man.'

Charlie unhooked his arm from Mandy's waist, 'Sorry, I didn't realise you two were an item.'

'You didn't realise Enis and I were an item either,' said Guy disapprovingly, 'you need to be more careful.'

'Sorry, I've just got divorced and I'm rather eager to find a new lady friend.'

'Over bloody eager, if you ask me,' mumbled Guy.

'Interesting that, Mandy and I are being divorced by our spouses. Perhaps you can give us some advice?'

'I'd love to but I think my friend Neil from ITV is ready to interview Enis now.'

Charlie grabbed Enis's arm and took her to the front of the shop where the TV camera was. Guy followed closely behind.

'Enis, this is Neil Halifax from ITV, he's going to ask you some questions about the tattoo parlour.'

'OK, I'm ready.'

'Stand still,' said Neil, 'while I adjust the

focus.'

Neil started to adjust the camera. 'OK, Enis, ready?'

Enis nodded.

'Now Enis, I understand your attempt to open a tattoo parlour in Linton has met with some local opposition.'

'Yes, nasty peoples spread lies. They produce leaflet which is rubbish and slander.'

'Yes, I have a copy of the leaflet here. The leaflet makes several allegations, which I'll run through now. It says you are not complying with environmental and health issues.'

'That is not true. I had councilman here last week, and he passed us flying colours.'

'It mentions worries about the safe disposal of needles and blood-stained tissues spreading AIDS.'

'Rubbish. Even before AIDS, tattooists very careful with waste products due to other diseases. Councilman was happy with our system.'

'It says you've not applied for planning permission for the shop.'

'I did not understand rules. Where I come from, shop is shop. But is done now and councilman says no problem in, how you say, change of use?'

'Yes, correct. The final thing the leaflet asks is this. Is allowing a tattoo parlour the commercial direction we would want Linton to take? Don't you think that is pure snobbery?'

'Absolutely. But all sorts of people have tattoos now, it is becoming more popular.'

'And worst of all, the producers of this leaflet haven't signed it. What do you think about that?'

'They are cowards, why not come and ask if they got worries? I could put minds at rest.'

'Well thank you for talking to us Enis and good luck with the shop.'

'No, thank you for taking time to visit and film.'

Neil stopped the camera. 'OK, that's a wrap. I'll do some establishing shots outside and get back to the studio. It will be on the six o'clock news tonight.'

'Thank you so much, Neil, and thank you, Charlie, for bringing him with you.'

'I'll put my copy in later,' said Charlie, 'and the story should be in some National papers tomorrow.'

'That is so good, Charlie. Thank you again. You must come to the flying club tonight, so I can thank you properly.'

'Ooh, that sounds interesting.'

'She means to buy you a drink.'

'Oh right, of course, love to. Roger, Mandy, if you two are there, I can probably give you some advice about your divorces.'

'Look forward to it.' Roger turned to Mandy, 'Look I'll catch you back at the club, I'm off to see a solicitor now.'

CHAPTER TWENTY

Roger walked into the Flight Training reception. Mandy was behind the desk.

'How did it go, Roger?'

'Well, good and bad news really. The good news is as I owned the house before we married, I won't need to split its value fifty-fifty with her. Quite a bit less he reckons.'

'What's the bad news?'

'The bad news is because we are married, she has a right to be in the house, although we can probably delay that for a while as she is shacked up with someone else. I left her solicitor's letter with my solicitor, and he's going to answer it.'

'But what happens to me if you have to let her back in?'

'I don't know. I didn't think to ask him. But I'll be damned if I'll let that happen. I explained we're all happy as we are, except Alison. Although I think she is happy living with Dan, she is determined to stop us from being happy. I told him to expedite the divorce, so I can get her out of my hair forever.'

'Let's hope he can keep her at bay.'

'Yes. Now, is Lewis around?'

'Yes, he's in his office.'

Roger knocked on the door and stuck his head in. 'The weather doesn't seem very pleasant but how about doing the instrument flying now Lewis?'

'Yes, OK. You don't need pleasant weather for instrument flying, instrument flying is what you do when the weather is unpleasant.'

'OK, well let's do it.'

Lewis came out of his office. 'Right. Mandy, can you book us out in Hotel-Tango please.'

'Will do,' replied Mandy.

Roger and Lewis took off, climbed to three thousand feet, and found a relatively clear area to fly in.

'OK Roger, so we are flying straight and

level now and I want you to look at the artificial horizon. This is your master instrument. Observe how the dot in the centre is just below the horizon, as the nose of our aircraft is, and the bars to the left and right represent our wings, which are level. Now if we turn to the left, the right wing on the artificial horizon is raised and the left wing is lowered, and a right turn produces the opposite effect. If we lower or raise the nose like this, you can again see the artificial horizon mimics the real horizon visible out of the window. Now you have control, make various manoeuvres and satisfy yourself you don't need to look out of the window, you can observe the same effects on the artificial horizon.'

Roger tried some turning, climbing, and descending to see the effect.

'Now try a turn to the left and notice how your other instruments confirm what you are doing. Notice the turn and slip indicator is indicating a turn to the left, and, as you haven't pulled back on the control column to allow for the reduced lift during the turn, the aircraft is descending as indicated by the artificial horizon and confirmed by the altitude reducing on the altimeter, the airspeed increasing on the airspeed indicator and descent indicated on the vertical speed indicator.'

'You need to develop a scan, from the master instrument out to the other instruments to confirm you are getting the results you desire, then quickly back to the master instrument. Now I'll give you some manoeuvres to do and you try to complete them without looking out of the window. Don't forget to scan.'

Lewis gave Roger some manoeuvres and Roger did his best to follow.

'Not bad Roger, the scan will come with practise. Don't fixate on any one instrument.'

'What happens if the artificial horizon should fail?'

'Good question and that's why you are learning how the other instruments confirm what the artificial horizon is telling you. It's far more likely the suction will fail and will take out the direction indicator as well. It's perfectly possible, although a little more difficult, to fly on a limited panel. You will need to coordinate your turns with reference to the compass and that throws up some other problems. Now I'll cover up the artificial horizon but leave the direction indicator. Use the turn and slip to coordinate turns with the compass and the altimeter and vertical speed indicator for altitude.'

Roger tried to follow Lewis's instructions but with less success this time.

'More difficult, isn't it? Did you notice how you overshot the turns onto north and undershot the turns onto south? Remember to roll out early on turns onto north and late on turns onto south, allow around 30 degrees of error. This is a problem with compasses. A better way is to use timed turns. See those marks on the turn and slip indicator? It indicates the roll rate for a rate-one turn or three degrees of turn a second. Using those marks to control the amount of bank, you can turn onto any heading at a change of three degrees a second, so to turn ninety degrees, you turn for ninety divided by three or thirty seconds. We'll give it a try.'

Lewis gave Roger several turns to complete, and Roger used his stopwatch to time them. 'That's far easier,' said Roger.

'OK,' said Lewis, 'On the way back to the airfield, I'll put the aircraft into some unusual attitudes and you can use the instruments to return it to straight and level flight.'

CHAPTER TWENTY-ONE

Roger and Lewis walked back into Flight Training reception.

'Well done Roger, only your GFT to complete now. I got hold of Mr Rich, err I mean Dave, and he said he might pop into the club tonight. You can sort out a time with him when you are both available and get your GFT done. I presume you will be in the club tonight?'

'Oh yes, I'll be there. I'm going over there now.'

'OK, well I'll leave it with you. If you want to go with him Mandy, I'll hold the fort. We've got nothing booked.' Lewis went back into his office and shut the door.

'Well, what a turn-up. Come on Mandy let's go. I don't know what time Charlie

Garth is coming but it should be a good night tonight!'

Roger and Mandy left reception and crossed the road over to the club. As they walked in Roger noticed that Kingsley had a big smile on his face, which obviously meant Phil, Mr Menu wasn't around. He spotted Guy standing at the bar, and they went over.

'Hello, Guy,'

'Hello Roger, been flying again?'

'Yes, been doing some instrument flying.'

'Oh good,' said Guy looking totally nonplussed. 'I say, Kingsley seems on good form tonight.'

'Yes, I think that's because Mr Menu isn't in. I caught him last night, winding Kingsley up with a menu from some posh hotel in Paris. Kingsley said those sorts of dishes weren't appropriate for a flying club and his home-made pies were what the punters wanted.'

'Home-made pies?' said Mandy, 'What home-made pies? His pies aren't home-made. I see the Brake Brothers van call twice a week while I'm working in reception. That's where his home-made pies come from.'

92

'Really? Well, I suppose they could still be called home-made pies if someone at Brake Brothers made them at home.'

'No, Brake Brothers owns that big factory on the industrial estate. That's where all their stuff is made.'

'Oh, so perhaps he's been telling us porkies. He does seem rather pretentious, doesn't he, what with his menu descriptions such as "a medley of lightly roasted vegetables"'

'Well pretty standard for the restaurant trade, isn't it? The more adjectives and big words you can squeeze on the menu, the more you can charge.'

'I asked him for a plate of chips the other night,' said Guy, 'and he said sorry, he only had French fries. Pretentious or what?'

'Who's pretentious?' asked a voice.

'Oh hello, George. Kingsley is. Apparently, his home-made pies aren't.'

'Aren't what?'

'Home-made. Mandy sees the Brake Brothers van call twice a week.'

'Oh. I've not tried one. His peppered steaks are my favourite, talking of which, I must order one. My wife has me on a diet. Kingsley, a pint and a peppered steak please.' He looked around at his companions. 'You've not got any drinks, is it Steve's round? Better get this lot a drink as well, Kingsley.'

'Thanks, George.'

'So Roger, how did the instrument flying go today?'

'Fine thanks. I found it fascinating and I can't wait to do more. If I pass my GFT, I'll start doing a night rating and so on.'

'Has Lewis arranged your GFT with Mr Rich?'

'Not quite. He said he may come in here tonight, and we can agree on a mutually convenient time to do it.'

'Oh, I do hope so. Haven't seen him for quite a while now.'

CHAPTER TWENTY-TWO

There was some commotion as Guy and Enis ran into the bar at breakneck speed, closely followed by Charlie Garth. 'Fidel, Kingsley, quick can you put the ITV news on please,' shouted Guy, 'Enis's interview should be on.'

Fidel found the remote and switched the TV on. The first picture showed the outside of Enis's tattoo parlour. The bar went quiet as everyone watched the ensuing interview of Enis on the TV. When the interview had finished, most people turned back to what they were doing, until Neil Halifax continued.

'Since I interviewed Enis this morning, we've followed up on several leads to identify who was responsible for producing the leaflet. Luckily, one copy had been photocopied by mistake onto the back of a piece of letter-headed notepaper. With the assistance of a local newspaper reporter, Charlie Garth, we went first to a local business and ultimately to this house in Linton.' A shot of a house appeared on the screen.

'That's your house, Roger,' said Mandy in a hushed voice. Roger's jaw dropped, as did his pint. The glass smashed on the floor. Roger made a sort of gurgling noise. 'W what..?'

Neil Halifax continued, 'Unfortunately, we got no answer when we called there earlier today, but we did manage to track the perpetrator to this house in Fleawick.' Another house appeared on the screen.

'And that's your house, Mandy,' said Roger. It was Mandy's jaw's turn to drop. Fortunately, she managed to keep hold of her G and T.

On the screen, a couple appeared at the door. Neil Halifax shoved a microphone towards the woman and showed her a copy of the leaflet. 'Alison Moore, I understand that you are responsible for producing this leaflet against the tattoo parlour in Linton.

But all the information contained in the leaflet is wrong and the owner has refuted it all. I wonder if you would care to comment?'

Alison stared at the camera like a startled rabbit, then she suddenly reclaimed some poise and stepped forward to the camera. 'The tattoo parlour is not in keeping with a small market town like Linton. It will attract hordes of dirty, greasy Hells' Angels on noisy motorbikes, not to mention the possibility of contaminated needles and tissues lying in the streets. It's just something Linton can do without.'

Alison turned, went back into the house and slammed the door. The camera turned on to Neil Halifax. 'Well viewers, I think we can safely say snobbery is alive and kicking in Linton. Neil Halifax for ITV News, in Linton.'

Fidel switched the TV off from behind the bar and then brought a mop and bucket round to where Roger dropped his pint on the floor and started mopping up. Enis and Guy looked accusingly at Roger. 'Alison Moore, I presume is your wife?' asked Guy.

'Yes, she is but I had no idea she was behind the leaflet. I'm not living with her anymore, and we're getting a divorce. But I'm not surprised, she is a dreadful snob. I can only apologise.'

'And Mandy, I presume the chap she was with on the TV must be your husband?'

'Yes, but likewise, I had no idea of what they were up to. I'm not living with him, and we're getting a divorce too.'

'So Charlie, how did you track her down?' asked Roger.

'Easy, the leaflet printed on the back of some letterhead led me to her firm. When I mentioned ITV, they couldn't shop Mrs Moore fast enough. Then I found no one was at home, so I went back and one of her workmates told me where I could find her. I passed it on to Neil.'

'Quite the detective aren't you. So you write articles for the national papers?'

'Yes, as well as the local ones. I like to cause a bit of controversy in the locals, I once wrote that giving pensioners bus passes was responsible for the decline in people using public transport, as nowadays most buses smelt slightly of wee.'

'Yes, I can see how that would upset a few old folks.'

'Certainly did. An old woman appeared

in my local pub one night. She told people she was going to punch me when I came in. A mate sent me a text to tip me off, but I was working in London at the time.'

'So have you always been a wind-up merchant?'

'Well growing up in the Littleborough area of Lancashire in the fifties, there wasn't much else to keep us amused. So I sort of grew up like it. On April 1st one year, I tried to get a story published under the headline "Lord Mountbatten had dandruff."'

'Wasn't he blown up on his boat by the IRA? Why dandruff?'

'Well, the police report said that after the explosion they had found his head and shoulders on the beach.'

'Oh, dear! That's dreadful! Surely they didn't print it?'

'No, the editor spotted it and threw it out.'

'I'm not surprised. It really was in awfully bad taste.'

'Well I subscribe to Oscar Wilde's theory that nothing is in bad taste as long as it's funny,' said Charlie, 'now I think someone offered to buy me a drink.'

'Yes,' said Enis, 'I want to buy you all drink for supporting me today. Fidel drinks please!'

CHAPTER TWENTY-THREE

'Now Roger, about our next flight,' said George, 'We've two seats spare, any ideas on filling them?'

'None at all.'

'Is this a trip somewhere in a light aircraft?' asked Charlie, 'If so, may I join you? I've got lots of holidays owing and nothing much to do. I've always wanted to fly in a light aircraft.'

'Yes of course you can,' replied Roger. 'One seat to go, George.'

'OK, I think I can sort it. A chap who works for me keeps asking. His name is Gary. I'm pretty sure he'll come. I'll phone him tonight.'

'Your steak is here, George,' said Kingsley and put a plate on the bar. George picked it up and went to a table.

'So you said you are divorced, Charlie?' asked Mandy.

'Yes, my wife sued me for divorce because she said I couldn't get an erection anymore. I thought I had good evidence to the contrary, but it didn't stand up in court. When the judge said we had to split the house fifty-fifty, it seemed quite fair at the time. Unfortunately, though, I got the outside. Divorce laws in this country are very much biased in favour of the woman.'

'Good to know,' said Mandy.

'I'm not so sure about that,' said Roger.

'My advice is for you to find a good solicitor, Roger. After all, the result of divorce usually depends on who has the best solicitor. Did you know that while only ten per cent of husbands kiss their wives goodbye when leaving the house, ninety per cent of husbands kiss their house goodbye when leaving their wife?'

'No, I didn't but it seems believable. So what went wrong in your marriage, Charlie?'

'Well, she was quite a bit older than me and the menopause is what went wrong. I think there is an "n" missing in menopause, it should be called the menonpause. After women go through it, they tend to put men on pause, and then eventually stop. Regular sex is the first thing that suffers. I read that those men who make love twice a week live 12 years longer than men who are celibate. So I said to my wife, "You're trying to kill me, aren't you?" Then of course the trust goes, and they become paranoid you're shagging someone else. She asked me, "Have you been having sex behind my back?" I said, "Well who the hell did you think it was and if you were in any doubt, you could have turned around and looked."'

'Do you find you miss her?'

'Well, maybe a bit. I mean the sex now is just as disappointing, but the dishes are really starting to pile up in the sink.'

'Well, good luck in finding a replacement.'

'She did say she still wanted us to be friends after the divorce but I thought no, that's like kidnappers asking you to keep in touch after releasing you.' Charlie looked around the bar. 'Not too much crumpet on offer in here is there?'

'It will liven up a bit later when the crews come in.'

'You should come here on a Sunday

night,' said Guy.

'He just got rid of one older woman,' said Roger, 'he doesn't want to replace her with a Granny.'

Charlie laughed. 'Well, to be honest, I'm not too fussy, as long as she's still got a pulse. So far, all the decent-looking birds I've seen here are taken. Enis is the epitome of an eastern European beauty and Mandy looks like a dead heat in a Zeppelin race.'

'You try to remember they're both spoken for Charlie,' said Guy, 'and keep your hands to yourself.'

'Oh I will Guy, but you need to remember, women are like roads. The more curves they have, the more dangerous they can be.'

CHAPTER TWENTY-FOUR

George returned to the bar and put his plate down. 'Lovely as usual, Kingsley. Thank you very much.'

'Glad you enjoyed it, George. Now there's a well-to-do looking chap at the other end of the bar asking for Roger, but he looks a bit like a debt collector, so I didn't like to point Roger out.'

George looked down the bar and laughed. 'No, that's Mr Rich, he's absolutely fine. He's here to arrange a flying test with Roger. Leave it to me, I'll introduce him.'

George went to the end of the bar, 'Hello Rich, how are you?'

'Hello George, fine thanks. I'm here to meet Roger about a GFT.'

'Yes, I know. Come with me and I'll

introduce you.' He took Dave over to Roger.

'Roger, I'd like you to meet Mr Rich, err Dave Norris, he's here to arrange your GFT. Dave, Roger, Roger, Dave.'

'Hello, Roger. I hear good things about you from Lewis.'

'Hello, Dave. Thanks for coming in. Would you like a drink?'

'Yes, a pint please.'

'Kingsley, can I have a pint for Dave please, and whatever anyone else wants?'

'Thanks, Roger. Now I can't stop long so when would you like to do your GFT? I'm fairly flexible for the next few days.'

'Well ASAP really.'

'Well, I'm free tomorrow lunchtime.'

'Yes, that would be great, Dave. Midday?'

'OK, midday it is. I'll see you then.'

George took Dave by the arm. 'Great, now you've sorted that out, come over here, there are some old faces you haven't seen in ages.'

'Seems a nice chap,' said Charlie.

Roger heard some familiar squawking and turned as Captain Slack and his crew came in the door, led by Seymour and Kyle.

'Oh hello, Roger, how..'

'Hello Kyle,' interrupted Roger, 'how

bona to vada your dolly old eek.'

'Oh he's learning all the Polari now,' squawked Seymour, 'I think he's on the turn.'

'I bloody hope not,' said Mandy.

Kyle and Seymour went to the bar followed by the rest of the crew. Sandy threw a glance in Roger's direction but when she saw Mandy was with him, she scowled, shook her head and walked on.

'I say, now that's crumpet!' said Charlie a bit too loud. Sandy looked back and smiled sweetly at him.

'If you lot will excuse me, I think I'll go and chat that up,' and shot off after Sandy.

'He's keen,' said Guy, 'Now it's almost time for me to start my disco.'

'Oh, is that the time,' said Roger, looking at his watch. 'I think we'll finish these drinks and go Mandy. That instrument flying has made me quite exhausted.'

'Are you two off?' asked George rejoining the group. 'Dave says goodbye, Roger, he'll meet you at midday. Good luck with your GFT.'

'Thanks, George.'

'Now about our next flight, I rang Gary, and he's on. So we have a full house.'

'Brilliant George. Now we must be off.'

Roger and Mandy were walking towards the door when Charlie rushed up. 'I think I've pulled Roger. Apparently, her flatmate is away, and she's desperate to move some furniture, so she's asked me to give her a hand tonight.'

Roger looked shocked. 'Err, that's great Charlie.'

As they went through the door, Roger whispered to Mandy, 'She's definitely is desperate.'

'Take no notice, Roger. She's just doing it to get her own back on you.'

CHAPTER TWENTY-FIVE

Roger and Mandy were enjoying breakfast. Roger was deep in thought and not saying much.

'Cheer up Roger,' said Mandy.

'Oh,' Roger looked up. 'Sorry.'

'What are you thinking about? Your GFT?'

'Err yes,' lied Roger. He was actually thinking about Charlie and Sandy, and how he had missed out. *If Charlie's shagged her, he'll be insufferable.*

'Don't worry, Roger. I'm sure you'll pass. Lewis always speaks highly of your flying abilities.'

'I do hope so. I love flying and I'm keen to do much more. Oh, the postman.'

Roger got up and went to the front door,

bent down and retrieved the letter. 'Another solicitor's letter but this one is from mine. It's a copy of the letter he's sent to Alison's solicitor.'

Roger sat down and started reading. He smiled to himself. 'Yes, that's good. That's told her!'

'What does he say?'

'He points out she's committed adultery as well, so we are both in the wrong. And he goes on to point out as she moved in with her lover, that makes her a concubine as well.'

Roger continued reading, 'He goes on to say the divorce won't be contested, but as I owned the house before we married, she can't expect the court to make a 50/50 settlement.'

Roger chuckled. 'And in the last paragraph, he says he understands all other parties are happy with the current living arrangements, so she would be foolish to try to take possession of the property and cause unpleasantness which a divorce court may look upon unfavourably.'

Mandy smiled. 'I must say he has a way with words.'

'Yes, but if I know Alison, she won't take

a blind bit of notice of the letter. She always thinks she knows best.'

'What do you think she will do?'

'I've no idea.'

'OK, well I must go to work. You won't be in until midday I suppose?'

'Yes, I thought I'd brush up my knowledge on a few points before my GFT.'

'OK, I'll see you later.'

'Bye Mandy, yes I'll be there before midday.'

Mandy got up and went out the front door. She closed it quietly behind her.

CHAPTER TWENTY-SIX

Roger walked into the Flight Training reception. Mandy was behind the counter.

'Hello, Mandy. Is Mr Rich here yet?'

'Yes, he's been here a while. He's in the office with Lewis and Jane.'

Roger went to the office door and knocked.

'Come in.'

Roger opened the door. 'Hello, all. Dave, I'm ready for my GFT when you are. I'll be out here with Mandy when you're ready.' He shut the door.

A few minutes later, the door opened and Dave emerged.

'OK Roger, I'm ready.'

'Mandy, can you book us out in Hotel-Tango please.'

'Will do.'

Roger and Dave left reception and walked through the fence towards Hotel-Tango. Roger went around the aircraft and conducted a pre-flight check while Dave watched. They got into the aircraft and shut the doors.

'Now Dave,' said Roger, 'which pocket is your wallet in?'

'What?'

'Which pocket? I need to do a weight and balance check.'

'Roger, what are you on about?'

'George said you catch unwary students out if they don't take your incredibly heavy wallet into account before flying. He said I must do a proper weight and balance check or I could fail my GFT.'

'Roger, George was winding you up. My wallet probably weighs a lot less than yours.'

'But you are known as Mr Rich. It seemed the correct thing to do in the circumstances, what with you owning a chain of garages. Word is that you used to live in a country cottage and now you live in a millionaires mansion. People say that's where "The Game of Life" got their ideas from.'

'Roger, it's all a bit of banter between

friends, don't take it so seriously. You categorically do not need to do a weight and balance check, alright? I can see from your training record that you know how to do it. Now please, start the engine, call the tower and let's get this GFT started.'

Roger started the engine, checked the oil pressure, then called the tower.

'Linton Tower, Hotel Tango request taxi for local flight.'

'Hello Roger, good luck with your GFT,' said a familiar voice, 'Clear taxi for the holding point two-six, QNH One Zero One Five.'

'Thanks, Malcolm, clear taxi for the holding point two-six, One Zero One Five.'

'Let's hope the PTT switch doesn't stick on this flight,' said Dave.

'Oh, you know about that, do you?'

'Of course Roger. Your fame has spread far and wide, about as far and wide as that recording has, to be precise.'

'Indeed. I was up at Leicester on my qualifying cross-country and the whole airfield stopped and came out to meet me!'

'Well, all part of the fun of flying. A great community built on hard work, humour, alcohol and a distinct dislike of political correctness. I understand you and Mandy are an item now. I don't want to speak out of turn but you do realise she's been around the block a bit?'

'Yes of course I do. But only because she was looking for some sort of happiness. I was as well. Now we both seem to have found what we were looking for.'

'Well, I'm very pleased to hear that Roger. Good luck to you both.'

Roger reached the holding point and was cleared for take-off. He took off and was climbing to a thousand feet when Dave suddenly pulled the throttle back and prodded the PTT button, 'Hotel-Tango, practise engine failure.'

'Roger Hotel-Tango, call climbing away,' replied Malcolm.

Roger looked down and spotted the field he had used before when training. He turned the aircraft towards it and trimmed for best glide speed. 'I'll go for that long field there,' he said and went about the practise shutdown procedure, just touching the controls he would have to operate in a real situation.

'OK,' said Dave, 'you would definitely make it to the field. Climb away to three thousand feet.' He pressed the PTT button, 'Hotel-Tango, climbing away.'

Roger climbed the aircraft to three thousand feet and Dave began to put him through his paces. Stalls, steep turns, climbs and descents.

'OK, that's all fine, give Linton a call, and we'll go back and hit the circuit.'

CHAPTER TWENTY-SEVEN

Roger pressed the PTT switch. 'Linton Tower, Hotel-Tango. We'd like to rejoin the circuit please.'

'Roger Hotel-Tango. Runway two-six, left-hand circuits, QFE niner-niner-eight, wind two-five-zero at ten knots. Call on finals.'

'Two-six, left-hand circuits, niner-niner-eight, call on finals, Hotel-Tango.'

Roger headed back to Linton and joined the circuit.

'Hotel-Tango, finals.'

'Roger Hotel-Tango, clear land or touch-and-go, wind two-five-zero at ten knots.'

'Cleared touch-and-go, Hotel-Tango.'

Roger landed the aircraft on the numbers, opened the throttle and sped down the runway. Hotel-Tango leapt back into the air and climbed away. At five hundred feet, Roger started a climbing turn to the left.

Suddenly Dave started sniffing. 'Can you smell smoke?'

Roger sniffed. 'Yes, I can and I think it's getting worse.'

'Look, there's smoke coming out from under the dashboard.'

'Dave, why don't you grab the fire extinguisher from behind the seat while I declare an emergency?'

Roger pressed the PTT button. 'Mayday, mayday, mayday, Hotel-Tango we have a fire on board, request assistance.'

Down in the tower, Malcolm was in two minds. 'Roger Hotel-Tango, confirm this is a practise mayday?'

'No Malcolm, definitely not a practise, we are on fire!'

'Roger Hotel-Tango. There is no traffic in the circuit or on the ground. The airfield is yours, all runways are available. I'll alert the fire service, good luck Roger.' Malcolm pressed the alarm button to bring out the airfield fire service.

Inside Hotel-Tango, Dave grabbed the fire extinguisher and stood ready to douse any flames inside the cockpit. Roger had just turned the aircraft on to the downwind leg when flames appeared from underneath the engine cowling.

'It must be a fuel leak,' said Roger, 'we're at seven hundred feet in close proximity to the airfield, so I'm turning the fuel and ignition off. I'm sure I can't miss the airfield from here.'

'Good idea!' agreed Dave.

Roger turned the fuel and ignition off and continued on the downwind leg. He trimmed for best glide speed. His eyes darted between the altimeter and the runway to judge the best place turn base leg. He expected the flames to diminish once the fuel flow stopped, but they continued and the airflow was directing them into the cabin.

'Hotel-Tango, base leg.'

'Roger Hotel-Tango, the emergency services are out and will meet you wherever you land.'

Roger didn't answer, the flames were now entering the cabin and Dave was using the extinguisher.

'I'll side-slip to divert the flames,' said Roger, 'We'll lose height I know, but that's better than being incinerated.'

Roger lowered the left wing so the flames went to the right of the cabin. They crossed the airfield perimeter fence, losing height. Roger looked at the altimeter and the airspeed indicator.

'I can't turn for the runway now Dave, we won't make it. I can make the apron though. Can you unlatch the doors please?'

He reversed the sideslip and aimed at the apron. Luckily all the aircraft had parked well back. As they reached the ground, he pulled back on the control column to arrest the descent and landed with a bump. He quickly applied the brakes and brought the aircraft to a shuddering halt. They both got out of the aircraft as fast as they could, nearly colliding with a small fire appliance that pulled up alongside.

A fireman was out and unreeling a hose in an instant. He pulled it to the front of Hotel-Tango and directed the flow through the front cowling. After a few seconds, the flames stopped and were replaced by smoke and steam.

'Lucky escape,' said the fireman.

Lewis and Mandy ran across the apron and joined them. Mandy flung her arms around Roger. 'Are you OK Roger?' she said breathlessly.

'Yes I'm fine and Dave is fine, thanks. Mind you, if we were in the air much longer it might have been a different story.'

'What do you think caused the fire?' asked Lewis.

'I'm not sure. I thought it was maybe a fractured fuel line but turning the fuel off didn't seem to make much difference.'

'Maybe the fuel set other things alight,' suggested Dave.

'Well I think we will find out in due course,' said Lewis, 'the tower will have rung the Accident Investigation Branch, and they'll be keen to find the answer.'

'More importantly Roger,' said Mandy, 'did you pass your GFT?'

'Oh I don't know,' Roger turned to Dave, 'what do you think?'

'Yes, you passed with flying colours Roger. You handled that emergency correctly and professionally and the way you used side-slip to keep the flames away from the cabin was inspirational. Consider yourself a Private Pilot!'

CHAPTER TWENTY-EIGHT

Roger, Mandy, Dave and Lewis burst into the flying club bar. The place was busy and Piers was alone behind the bar with no sign of Kingsley or Fidel anywhere.

Roger spotted George, who was standing at the bar. 'Hello George, bit early for you isn't it?'

'Hello, Roger. Just popped in to see how your GFT went but I hear you had a fire?'

'News travels fast. How did you know?'

'Oh, Mark over there told me. He was the fireman that put your fire out.'

Roger looked down the bar at Mark. 'I thought I recognised him when he jumped out of the fire engine. I realise now I've seen him in here before.'

'Yes he used to be a fireman with the

122

county brigade, but he's retired now on one of those gold-plated public service pensions we would all give our right arms for. But give him his due, he's not used it to buy a castle in France like a lot of his mates, he's volunteered to help keep the airport covered for fire personnel. He's a nice chap, he doesn't get paid for what he does but then again he obviously doesn't need any extra money, does he?'

'Probably not.'

'Anyway, did you pass OK?'

'Yes, I did, thank you and the drinks are on me when Piers has a moment. He looks rushed off his feet.'

'Congratulations Roger. I knew you would pass OK. Now there's something I want to talk to you about..'

'Yes Roger, what can I get you?' interrupted Piers.

'Drinks all round on me please, including your good self Piers. You look knackered, where are Kingsley and Fidel?'

'Oh, they've gone away for a few days, anniversary or something. When I said I would look after the place, I didn't realise it would be so busy.'

'Looks like you need some help.'

'Yes, well I do. Luckily I know a young chap called Daniel whose Dad runs a local pub, he might help me out. I will be contacting him, assuming I last this evening out.'

'OK, can you make sure Mark the fireman at the end of the bar gets a drink please?'

'OK, Roger will do. I guess it was Mark who put your fire out?'

'Yes, it was.'

Roger turned to the bar. 'Ladies and Gentlemen, Having just passed my GFT, I'd like to buy you all a drink.'

A big cheer went up and people surged forward to the bar. Piers looked at Roger and shook his head. 'Thanks for that, Roger.'

Roger turned to George, 'What did you want to talk to me about?'

'Well now you've passed, why don't we think about forming a group to buy our own aircraft?'

'Sounds interesting, what sort had you in mind?'

'Well, a six-seater, something like a Piper Lance, with a three hundred horsepower engine. It'll do one hundred and fifty knots and there will be lots of avionics on board to make those long flights a lot easier.'

'OK, I like the sound of that. How many people do you think we need?'

'Well eight to about ten maximum, I thought to make the capital outlay sensible. Any more than ten and you'll never be able to fly the bloody thing.'

'OK. Anyone else in mind?'

'Yes, there are a few pilots who come in here that hire the club aircraft. Morris, he's a structural engineer, so he must be loaded, and he's friendly with Keith who is an estate agent, so he's got plenty as well. Also, Alan, who runs some wholesale business and Fred who is an acoustic engineer. That's six..'

'Roger, sorry to interrupt but I'm off now,' said Dave, 'I've given Lewis all the necessary paperwork so you can apply for your licence. It was good to fly with you this afternoon and I'm sure you'll go far with your flying.'

'Thanks, Dave. Talking of going far, we were talking about getting a group together to buy a six-seater. Would you be interested?'

'Yes, funnily enough, my friend Jay and I've been talking about that sort of purchase for taking our families away. Yes, Roger, I am interested, you have my number, so please keep me in the picture. Bye for now.'

'Will do. Hope to see you soon.'

'That's eight possibles then,' said George as Dave left the club, 'given time, I can probably think of more.'

CHAPTER TWENTY-NINE

'Now I'm absolutely starving,' said George, 'I came straight here to see how your GFT went and didn't go home for my tea, so I think one of Kingsley's peppered steaks is in order.'

'The boys are away, some anniversary thing according to Piers,' said Roger.

George looked shocked. He attracted Piers's attention. 'Piers, who is cooking the food tonight?'

'No food tonight I'm afraid George, the boys are away.'

'But I've not eaten. Can't you rustle me up a peppered steak?'

'Sorry George, I'm rushed off my feet behind the bar. But I do know a very good barman-cum-chef called Daniel, I'll endeavour to bring him with me for the rest of the boy's absence.'

'Thanks, Piers, but that doesn't help my stomach now, and we'll be away for the next couple of days in Gibraltar.'

'Well, I'm afraid I can only offer you crisps or peanuts.'

'No thanks, I'll have to think of something else.'

'Excuse me a moment George,' said Roger, 'I must go and thank Mark for his help this afternoon.'

Roger went down to the end of the bar where Mark was standing. He held out his hand. 'Hello Mark, I'm Roger, I wanted to thank you for your sterling help with the fire this afternoon.'

'Oh no problem Roger, it's what we are here for. I'm just glad you got it down in time before anyone got hurt.'

'Any idea what caused the fire?'

'Not for me to say, Roger. The aircraft is in a secure area and the AIB chaps will be down tomorrow. They'll sort the cause out, they do it every day. But off the record, I think maybe a fuel line fracture.'

'But when I turned the fuel off, it still kept going.'

'Yes, but if it had been spraying fuel everywhere, then that's probably what kept burning.'

'OK, well thanks again for your help, Mark. The drinks are on me tonight, so make sure you grab another one.'

'Thanks, Roger. Will do.'

Roger walked back to where he had left George but George wasn't there. He looked around the club and saw George sitting at a table with two chaps, deep in conversation.

He headed back to where he had left Mandy. 'Sorry, I'm neglecting you, Mandy.'

'Oh, that's alright Roger. This is your night to celebrate. I'm so pleased for you, you are now a pilot!'

'Yes, and better than that, George and I are thinking of buying our own aircraft, with some other people of course.'

'Oh, that's brilliant Roger.'

'I think George is going around talking to prospective buyers now. He keeps moving from table to table. Oh, mind your back, here comes Guy and Charlie. Evening all.'

'Hello Roger,' said Guy, 'how did your test go?'

'Well apart from a fire onboard, pretty well. I passed. I'm now a pilot.'

'Oh well done. A fire?'

'Yes in the engine compartment, I managed to land it before it got too bad.'

'Can you give me all the details please Roger,' said Charlie, 'sounds like a good human interest story. It's how I make my living.'

'Not about pensioners pissing on buses then?'

'Well, that was more of a wind-up story.'

'So how did it go with Sandy last night? Did you move her furniture?'

'Oh yes. She's quite a girl when you get her going. We were moving her bed when somehow we both slipped and landed on top of each other. Well, one thing led to another and I ended up sh..'

'Err yes, spare us the gory details,' interrupted Roger, his face turning a sort of greenish-white.

'So thanks, Roger, if you had helped her out the other night, then I wouldn't have got my leg over.'

'Indeed,' said Mandy, frowning at Roger, 'But I'm sure Roger would.'

'So are you seeing her again?' asked Roger.

'Oh yes. Funnily enough, I mentioned we

were going on a trip to Gibraltar tomorrow and as luck would have it, she said their crew had been moved from the Lanzarote route on to the Linton to Gibraltar route. They fly out one day, stay overnight and fly back the next day. So they will be there in Gibraltar tomorrow night.'

'Wow, that is a coincidence,' said Roger, the colour starting to return to his face.

CHAPTER THIRTY

George rejoined the group.

'How did the aircraft sales pitch go?' asked Roger.

'Very well. Lots of interest. Morris, the structural engineer seemed keen, as did his mate the estate agent. Alan was undecided but thought he probably would. Also, a fire chap and a sound engineer I spoke to were interested.'

'Well, that's encouraging. When we return from Gibraltar, we must start looking around for a suitable aircraft to buy.'

'Yes, I thought a retractable six-seater with a bit of go, something like a Piper Lance or a Saratoga.'

'Sounds good but..'

'You bastard, George.'

They all spun around and there stood Steve, glowering in George's direction.

'What's up with you?' asked George.

'You bastard. We planned the flight to Gibraltar together, and now I hear you're taking Roger with you.'

'Yes, that's true. But I don't fly with you anymore since you ripped me off for the watch. Tough!'

'Yes, I know. But I've always wanted to go to Gibraltar, so you could at least let me have a seat on the flight?'

'No, I can't. I'm afraid every seat is taken. Sorry.'

Steve went red, turned on his heels and walked away. 'You'll regret this,' he shouted, before storming out of the club.

The club had fallen silent as they listened to Steve ranting.

Mark the fireman came over. 'He sounded really upset. I hope he will be OK.'

'He brought it all on himself. Anyway, I'm absolutely famished, what with no food being available here. Let's all go down to the China Cottage for a Chinese meal. Who's up for that?'

'Yes, I've been wanting to try the China Cottage,' said Roger, 'but every time we've returned from a flight something prevented us. First, it was a black eye, then we got stuck and came back in the day. Anybody else?'

Guy and Charlie nodded. Mandy was hungry.

'OK, well there's no need for us to take four cars, so we'd better organise a taxi. Anyone got a number?'

'I've got a friend called Robert who is a taxi driver,' said Mark, 'I'll give him a ring.'

'Oh but there are five of us, we don't want to overload Robert's taxi and get him into trouble.'

'Oh, Robert won't mind. He isn't one for rules. He spends a lot of his time up at the carriage office, being bollocked for being rude to passengers, or not carrying their suitcases. I think he has a regular appointment!'

'He sounds like our man!'

Mark got on his mobile and a few minutes later a horn sounded in the car park.

'That will be Robert.'

They all went outside and climbed into the taxi.

'Are you not coming Mark?' asked Robert.

'No, I'm off home.'

'Going to tot up your pension, I suppose.'

Mark winced and walked off. 'Night all. Enjoy your meal.'

'Where to?'

'China Cottage, please.'

'What? South of the ring road at this time of night? You've got to be joking.'

'Is that a problem?'

Robert mumbled something to himself, then thought better of it.

'Oh alright. Give my regards to Suzy Wong.'

CHAPTER THIRTY-ONE

Robert dropped them off outside the China Cottage. 'If you need taking home, here's my card.'

They all walked into the restaurant and were met by Susie Wong.

'Hello George, where have you been flying to today?'

'Nowhere today, although we're off to Gibraltar tomorrow. Unfortunately, the flying club has no food tonight, so we're all starving.'

'Well come in. A table for five? I'm sure we can sort you all out.'

Suzy Wong showed them to a table, 'I'll get you some menus.'

'Where's Ken tonight?' asked George.

'Oh, he's in the kitchen cooking. Have you

brought any crabs or lobsters with you?'

'No, as I said, we haven't been flying today.'

'OK, well Ken will be round shortly to take your orders.'

Mandy looked at the menu. 'I don't really know what to eat.'

'Well if you all leave the ordering to me, I can guarantee you the best of what Ken can offer.'

Ken arrived from the kitchen. 'Harrow George, what you want? Usual or new usual?'

'Oh, the new usual please, for five.'

'New usual for five. OK,' said Ken and disappeared back into the kitchen.

'The new usual?' asked Guy, 'what's that all about?'

'Oh we've been coming here for years, and we more or less settled on what we all liked, so rather than ordering separately each time, we called it the usual. Then we thought we would change a few dishes, so that became the new usual.'

'Oh, I see.'

'He'll have to use his own seafood today. But the food is much tastier when we bring our own back, fresh from Jernsey.'

137

'I heard on the radio today that one in five people in the world is now Chinese,' said Charlie, looking accusingly at the other four sitting around the table. 'Now I'm sure it's not me, so which of you four is it?'

George laughed. 'If we're having a Chinese joke session, keep your voices down. Ken and Susie Wong might not find them funny.'

'OK,' said Mandy, in a hushed voice, 'I only remember a Chinese proverb. "Man who go through airport turnstile sideways is bound to Bangkok", obviously wouldn't apply to you Guy, you being so small in that department.'

'Perhaps you better ask Enis for confirmation of that view, Mandy, you might be very surprised. But if after sex you'd told me I had a small organ, I would say sorry, it's just not used to playing in a cathedral.'

'Now, now, people,' said George, as Mandy kicked Guy under the table, 'We're off on a long trip tomorrow. Let's keep it civil.'

'I know one,' said Roger, 'What does the Chinese government and Viagra have in common?'

'Don't know.'

'They've both been rigging elections for years.' Charlie laughed. 'Complete waste, all the money they spent inventing Viagra, far more cost-effective to have improved slimming tablets for women. Would have achieved exactly the same result but at a fraction of the cost.'

Suzy Wong appeared with bowls of food. 'I'll put all these in the middle of the table so you can help yourselves.'

CHAPTER THIRTY-TWO

'This Chinese grub is really tasty,' said Roger, as the bowls of food emptied rapidly, 'I'm glad we got here in the end.'

'Absolutely. These meatballs are the dog's bollocks,' said Guy putting another two on his plate.

'I wish you had told me earlier,' said Mandy, looking decidedly sickly.

'I think we'd better go back to the club and then home,' said George. 'We've got an early start tomorrow. I'll give Robert a ring.'

He got on his mobile and five minutes later they heard a toot outside. They split the bill between them and left the restaurant. The five climbed back into Robert's taxi.

'Where to?'

'Back to the club please.'

'What time in the morning, George,' asked Charlie.

'Be at the club at seven. It's an eight-hour flight with a short break in Biarritz when we stop to refuel. Is everyone OK with that?'

They all nodded.

'Gary will turn up at seven. Now you haven't met Gary before so be nice to him and don't stare.'

'What do you mean?'

'Nothing, just do as I say.'

'OK.'

'Oh, and duty-free. I nearly forgot. What do you all want?'

'Bottle of whisky,' said Charlie.

'Same for me,' said Guy.

'Bottle of Pernod,' said Roger, trying to look more sophisticated.

'Bottle of gin and some Paco Rabanne pure XS,' said Mandy.

'Mandy, isn't that the perfume with the snake around the bottle?'

'Yes, it is, Guy. Do you use it yourself?'

'No, I don't use perfume at all. After-shave yes. I just thought it funny how you are instantly attracted to anything that looks like a snake.'

'Your after-shave Guy, is it called "Wet

Gun-dog"?'

'No.'

'Well, that's certainly what it smells like.'

'Roger,' said Charlie, 'we need to talk about your engine fire, so I can get my copy off to the dailies.'

'Well, we'll have plenty of time to talk during the trip.'

Robert pulled up at the flying club and the five disembarked.

George paid Robert, and they were all making for their cars when Steve emerged from the club accompanied by Alan. He was obviously worse for alcohol.

'George!' he shouted, 'Alan's not going to buy into your aircraft, he's already bought one of his own!'

'Good for Alan,' replied George, and continued walking to his car.

'And we're going to do a Gibraltar trip ourselves.'

'Wonderful. Knowing your navigational skills though, I hope you can find it. Goodnight.'

'You cheeky bastard.'

George got in his car and drove off.

CHAPTER THIRTY-THREE

Roger and Mandy were enjoying breakfast.

'Well another fantastic night, thanks Roger, but we really should get more sleep.'

'Well, you can nod off in the back with Guy, Charlie and Gary. I've got to stay awake to help George and also to learn.'

'Yes, but I'm not looking forward to Guy being on his own. At least Enis used to tell him off when he got a bit much.'

'Well, I'll tell him to shut up if he gets too much.'

'Would you? Mind you, it shut him up on the last flight when my heel contacted his bollocks!'

Roger laughed. 'Probably best you fight your own battles by the sound of it.'

'And I wonder what George meant when he said we weren't to stare at Gary?'

'I don't know, but I'm sure we'll find out soon enough.'

The letterbox clattered and Roger went to pick up the post.

'Another solicitor's letter. Must be from Alison's.'

He opened the envelope and started to read.

'I was right. I said Alison would ignore the very sensible advice my solicitor gave her.'

'What is she saying, Roger?'

'She's still saying she wants possession of the house and intends to take it. And we're going to be away for a couple of days. But I can't call the trip off, too many people are relying on us. I suppose I could call the police and ask them to keep an eye on the place.'

'I don't think they like being involved in domestic disputes, Roger.'

'Yes, that's right.'

'But what would you do if you were here, Roger. It seems she has a legal right to be here, which is more than I do.'

Roger noticed a tear in Mandy's eye.

'Hey, don't worry. You mean more to me than a house. We'll just have to see what the situation is when we return. I promise I won't let you down.'

'Oh Roger.' Mandy put her arm around him and gave him a kiss.

'Talking of letting people down, we better pick up our cases and get off to the club. I can't wait to meet Gary.'

CHAPTER THIRTY-FOUR

Roger and Mandy walked into the flying club reception area. Charlie and Guy were there and George was in conversation with another chap.

'Morning all,' said Roger.

George turned round. 'Ah Roger, Mandy. I'd like you to meet Gary. Gary, this is Roger and Mandy.'

Gary turned around and extended his hand. 'Pleased to meet you both.'

'Pleased to meet .. you,' stuttered a rather shocked Roger.

'Err hello,' was all Mandy could manage.

They both tried to cover their surprise as they looked at Gary, remembering what George had said.

'Now I've already done the Gen-Decs and

collected the duty-free. Roger, shall we look at the weather and the route?'

George and Roger went into the self-briefing area and looked at the weather chart.

'Well that explains the weather here,' said Roger, 'and that cold front extends all the way down to Dinard so it will be a bit bumpy for a while, but afterwards it looks plain sailing all the way down to Gibraltar.'

'Yes,' agreed George, 'I prepared this flight plan all the way, using radio navaids, so it will give you invaluable experience when you start your IMC rating. Right, let's get going.'

They went back into reception, collected the others and walked out onto the airfield. 'Go to the aircraft, we'll join you after we've filed the flight plan.'

George and Roger went to the tower and climbed the stairs to the top. 'Hello Malcolm,' said Roger, 'do you ever go home?'

'Not a lot at the moment, I'm afraid. We are very short-staffed. Got over your bad experience yesterday, I hope?'

'Yes, thanks. Can you file this flight plan to Gibraltar, please?'

'Yes of course I can. I think someone else from the club is going to Gibraltar in a couple of days.'

'Who is that?'

'Alan I think. He was talking about it in the club last night.'

'What aircraft is he going to use?'

'His own, I think. He flew it in last night, look it's down there at the end of the row. A Cherokee Six, Golf-Lima-Sierra-Tango-Golf.'

'So Steve was serious in what he said last night,' said Roger.

'So was I,' said George, 'Neither of them has the experience to fly so far on their own.'

'Ah, I think I can throw some light on that,' said Malcolm, 'they were talking to Greg. He's going to go with them.'

George laughed.

'Who is Greg?' asked Roger.

'He's an instructor,' replied George, 'I knew they wouldn't have the bottle to go alone. Anyway, we must get going.'

'Bye Malcolm,'

CHAPTER THIRTY-FIVE

Oscar-November was bumping along at three thousand feet, in and out of cloud all the way from Linton to about Jersey before any hint of an improvement in the weather.

'Oh look, there's a little patch of blue sky over there,' said Roger.

'Huh, just about big enough to make a British Telecoms engineer a wallet,' said George.

They continued south across Dinard and Nantes and suddenly the clouds rolled back and the ground became bathed in sunshine.

'Look, there are the old submarine pens at La Rochelle,' said Roger, 'isn't that the place Black Bob is always going on about?'

'Yes, he's always waving his hand and saying La Rochelle and Condom.'

'I presume Condom is a place and not rubber johnny?'

'Yes, I think it is a small airfield somewhere in the Pyrenees. How are the passengers doing?'

Roger looked round. 'They are all fast asleep.'

They flew on south and landed at Biarritz, their refuelling stop. They climbed out of the aircraft and stretched their legs. A bowser drew up beside the aircraft and the driver stuck his head out of the window.

'Do you require fuel, Monsieur?'

'Yes please,' replied George.

'George, look at the sign on the back of the bowser,' whispered Roger, 'only Francs accepted. Have you got any Francs? I haven't any.'

'No, I haven't. I think that's a bloody cheek, considering it's got British Petroleum on the side of the lorry. British bloody petroleum. Don't say anything. Let him fill it up, and then he's a bit stuck. He can't take it out again, can he?'

Just then, a French customs official came up.

'Bon matin Monsieur. J'ai besoin de voir votre manifeste douanier et votre liste de passagers.'

George and Roger looked at each other blankly.

'Do you speak English?' asked Roger.

The customs official looked equally blank and repeated what he said.

'Bon matin Monsieur. J'ai besoin de voir votre manifeste douanier et votre liste de passagers.

The man putting the fuel into the aircraft looked up. 'He says he wants to know what duty-free you have and a copy of your passenger list.'

'Well, why didn't he say so?' George and handed the customs official copies of both. The official looked at them, counted the heads standing next to the aircraft, had a quick look inside, then saluted George and walked off.

'That will be nine hundred francs, Monsieur,' said the fuel man.

George took out his wallet and handed him ninety pounds.

The fuel man frowned and pointed to the notice on the bowser.

George shrugged his shoulders and pointed to the money.

Oscar-November took off from Biarritz

and flew in a circle to gain enough height to clear the mountain at Flight Level Nine-Zero.

'Did you know that Spain is the most boring place in the world you can fly over?' said George, 'Oh look, a bull ring in the middle of a small town and oh look, another bull ring in the middle of another small town, with bugger all in between.'

They flew on over Spain using VOR navaids, Pamplona, Barahona, Castejon, Bailen until the Mediterranean sea appeared in front of them. They contacted Malaga who passed them on to Gibraltar.

George put on his best Hooray Henry voice. 'Hello, Gibraltar, Golf-Zulu-Oscar-Oscar-November inbound to you from Biarritz.'

'Roger Oscar-November, you are number two to a 737.'

The controller gave radar vectors that took them across the Med and put them on a five-mile final approach for runway 27.

The sun was low in the sky and George was having trouble seeing where he was going, but at three miles the Rock hid the sun and made the landing much easier.

They all clambered out of the aircraft and

stretched their legs.

'Right everyone,' said George, 'photographs of us and the aircraft with the Rock in the background. Individuals and as a group.'

CHAPTER THIRTY-SIX

The six passed through the airport checks and walked outside.

'Wow, isn't it warm,' said Mandy, 'particularly as it's nearly Christmas.'

'Well you are on the Mediterranean Sea,' said George, 'North Africa is only fifteen miles away, and there is a southerly wind blowing the heat up from the Sahara Desert.'

'We are going to need two taxis to take us to the hotel,' said Charlie.

'I assume Sandy gave you the name of the hotel where the crews stay,' said Roger.

'Yes, she did. Said she was looking forward to seeing me again.'

Two taxis pulled on to the rank, so they bundled their suitcases into their boots.

'Your suitcase, George,' said Gary, 'you didn't tell me you were evacuated during the war.'

'What do you mean?'

'Well, that's the oldest looking suitcase I've ever seen, apart from in second world war films.'

'You cheeky bugger,' laughed George. 'Charlie, you've got the address, so you ride in the front taxi and the second one can just follow.'

There was a short delay as the road into Gibraltar crossed the airport runway and another aircraft was coming into land.

The taxis pulled up outside the hotel, and they went into reception.

'Three rooms, I think,' said George, 'one double and two twins. Charlie and Guy can share one of the twins, and I'll share one with Gary. I'll meet you all in the bar in one hour.'

They all went to their rooms.

Roger and Mandy were pleased with their room.

'Come and try the bed Mandy, you'll find it really comfortable.'

'Down boy, wait until later. I'm going to have a quick bath.'

'Can I join you? We could play submarines.'

'Submarines? What are you on about?'

'You have to find my submarine. But it's periscope usually gives the game away.'

Mandy laughed. 'Leave me alone. I just want to relax. It was no fun sitting in the back of that aircraft. I'm very stiff.'

You and me both, thought Roger.

In Guy and Charlie's room, an argument was in progress.

'So you are saying you actually shagged Sandy?' asked Guy.

'Yes, of course, I did.'

'I don't believe it. You?'

'Why not. She reckons I'm a looker. Second time in a week that I've been called a looker. Remember that woman in the Queen's Head last Thursday?'

'Indeed, but the actual word that woman used was voyeur, when she caught you staring at her tits.'

'OK, the same thing though isn't it?'

'No, it's not!'

In George and Gary's room. George was champing at the bit to get down to the bar for a drink.

'You go, George, I'll catch you up. I want

to phone the wife, let her know we got here alright.'

'OK Gary, I'll see you down there.'

CHAPTER THIRTY-SEVEN

George arrived in the bar first and was drinking his second pint when the others arrived. After a round of drinks had been ordered, Mandy looked around for Gary. 'George, where's Gary?'

'He's making a phone call to his wife, to let her know we got here safely.'

'Thank goodness you warned us, otherwise, I really would have been shocked. Those great bulging eyes!'

'I thought Marty Feldman had come back from the dead,' said Guy.

'How on earth did he get like that,' asked Roger, 'was he born like it?'

'No, he wasn't. I've been told two stories and I'm not sure which to believe. If you ask Gary, he'll tell you when he was three, his mother made him a box to stand on, so he could pee into the toilet. He could just lay his little willy and sack over the edge of the bowl. Unfortunately, one day the seat fell down.'

All the men winced at the thought. Even Mandy screwed her face up.

'And the other story?'

'Well I met one of his old school friends, and he told a completely different story. He said that Gary was playing with himself at the back of the class during a sex lesson. The teacher spotted him and slammed the desk lid down hard on his erection.'

Again all the men winced at the thought and Mandy screwed her face up again.

'Either story could be true and both could produce the same result. All we know is one of them caused his great bulging eyes. Anyway, here comes Gary now, so don't mention the subject again.'

Gary walked into the bar and came over.

'Did you get hold of your wife?' asked George.

'Yes, she's happy now she knows we're safe. So, Charlie, you said we were meeting some aircrew here, where are they?'

'Well, that depends on what time their

plane actually lands. I'm sure they'll be here soon.'

Later Roger heard a familiar squawk, and Captain Slack's crew came into the bar led by Seymour, who was hanging on to Kyle's arm.

He spotted Roger. 'Oh Kyle, look who's here. It's your Dilly boy.'

'Oh hello Roger,' shouted Kyle, 'How's your..'

'About the same as the last time you asked me that Kyle,' interrupted Roger, 'oh, and the time before that.'

Behind them came Captain Slack, Sandy and Beverley. Sandy's face brightened briefly as she caught sight of Roger but darkened again as she saw Mandy. Her eyes came to rest on Charlie, so she went over and gave him a kiss.

'Great fun the other night Charlie, thank you.'

'Thanks, Sandy,' said Charlie, 'it certainly was fun. Would you like a drink?'

Roger made a strange groaning noise until Mandy kicked his ankle. 'Stop groaning Roger, she's just winding you up again.'

CHAPTER THIRTY-EIGHT

Roger couldn't bear to watch, so he turned to Kyle and Seymour.

'I'm sure you must have a story for me, Kyle.'

'You only want me for my stories Roger.'

'So very true,' said Roger with a laugh.

'Well, I once worked for Air Lingus on the Dublin to Boston route. Due to a catering mix up, we only had 40 meals delivered to feed over a hundred passengers. So I reluctantly told the passengers of the mix-up and said if anyone was good enough to give up their meal so someone else could eat, they would receive free, unlimited drinks for the duration of our 5-hour flight.'

'Sounds reasonable,' said Roger.

'Indeed. But three hours later I had to make another announcement.'

'Oh? What?'

'If anyone is actually hungry, we still have all 40 meals available.'

Roger laughed. 'Yes, sounds like the Irish. Nothing is more important than alcohol.'

Meanwhile, Charlie and Guy sat down with Sandy and Beverley.

Guy was hoping to pull Beverley, and Charlie was looking forward to a repeat performance with Sandy.

In an effort to impress the girls, Guy and Charlie took turns telling jokes. But as the night wore on and alcohol took its toll, the jokes became more and more off colour. Unfortunately, they didn't notice the girls had stopped laughing.

'What's the difference between a Western girl and an Arab girl?' asked Guy, 'A Western girl gets stoned before she commits adultery.'

'What's the difference between an air hostess and a Kit Kat bar?' asked Charlie, 'You can't get more than four fingers in a Kit Kat Bar.'

With that, Beverley went bright red. She stood up and slapped Charlie across the face. 'You know I'm an air hostess. How could you say something like that? Come on, Sandy. Let's leave these reprobates to their filth.'

With that, the two girls got up and left the bar.

'Oh brilliant Charlie,' said Guy, 'well done!'

CHAPTER THIRTY-NINE

They all rolled down to breakfast at around nine o'clock. When Roger ordered three slices of toast, he smiled at Guy, remembering their little bet in Jersey.

'Any of those brown?' asked Guy mischievously.

'No, I thought you and Charlie might be on the brown toast, seeing as neither of you pulled last night.'

'You cheeky bugger.'

'Now what shall we do today?' asked George. 'I thought a walk around the town, take the cable car up the rock to see the views and the apes, then some lunch.'

'They are actually monkeys, not apes,' said Charlie, 'apes don't have tails.'

After breakfast, they met up outside the

hotel ready for their walk.

'What lovely hanging baskets,' remarked Gary, and they all turned to admire the hotel's display.

'Yes, I do love it when people take the trouble to make their buildings look nice,' said Charlie, and they walked off up the street.

'I've got trailing lobelia,' said Mandy.

Guy looked quite concerned. 'I thought you were walking a bit funny, Mandy. But with all that sex you have, it's bound to damage your equipment. Can't you get an operation on the NHS, rather than drag them around with you?'

They all stopped and looked at Guy in amazement.

'Guy, trailing lobelia is a plant you put into hanging baskets, you idiot,' explained Mandy, 'it's what I've got in mine at home.'

'Oh right,' said Guy, 'I thought..'

'Yes, we all know what you thought, Guy.'

They walked around the town and George spotted a photography shop offering same-day developing. 'I must get some film developed and printed,' and went into the shop.

'I can pick it all up later today,' he said when he returned.

They continued their walk around town.

'Although this place has been British since 1713,' said Charlie, 'there's an awful lot of Spanish influence on display.'

They stood looking at an open-fronted shop that only contained a mechanical bull. People would sit on it and pay the operator, who then caused the mechanical bull to twist and buck violently, in an effort to throw the rider off. They stood and watched several people attempt to stay on, but every one of them ended up in a heap on the floor.

'I think I would be fantastic at that,' said Charlie.

'Really?' scoffed Guy, 'why on earth do you think you could do that when everyone else ended up on the floor?'

'Well,' said Charlie with a smile, 'when I was on my honeymoon, the wife had whooping cough.'

They took the cable car up the Rock. They got out at the top and leaned on the railings.

'What a vi..,' said Mandy, and screamed as one of the monkeys jumped on her and started looking in her handbag.

'Relax, Mandy,' said George, 'he's just

looking for food.'

The monkey didn't find any, so it jumped down and went off to bother the next tourist. A whole troop of monkeys walked along the path behind them, including some very young ones.

'We didn't need to fly over a thousand miles to see monkeys,' said Guy, 'we could have stayed in the flying club. Doesn't that little one over there with the black beard remind you of Bob?'

'I wonder if it speaks better French,' said Roger.

'Let's go for a walk along the top of the Rock,' said George. 'There are some caves and tunnels to explore.'

CHAPTER FORTY

The six sat eating lunch outside a restaurant, overlooking the harbour.

'I still can't get over how hot it is for December,' said Mandy, 'is there a swimming pool here? I fancy a dip this afternoon.'

'Yes, I think I saw one this morning as we walked around,' said Roger.

'Shall we go for a while this afternoon?'

'Well I didn't bring any trunks, but I've got some shorts that'll do.'

Guy looked up at the Rock. 'Oh look. Something is on fire at the very top. See that stream of smoke?'

They all turned to look. 'Ah, I don't think that's smoke,' said Roger, 'I remember this from my PPL Meteorology textbook. That's called the Levanter, cloud caused by the wind blowing up the sheer eastern face of the Rock.'

'Yes the wind must have turned easterly,' said George, 'the air rises almost one and a half thousand feet and cools to below its dew point. That produces fog which billows like steam around the top of the Rock and makes it look like the back of a British Telecoms van at tea break.'

'So does anyone else want to go swimming?' asked Roger.

'I won't,' said George, 'I want to go on a tunnel tour that brings you out about halfway up the sheer face that overlooks the airfield. I'm told the view is great. I've also got to collect my pictures. I'll see you back in the bar.'

The other three decided to go with George, leaving Roger and Mandy to go it alone. They collected their costumes from the hotel and found a quiet spot in the sun at the pool. They were having their second swim when suddenly a klaxon went off. A man ran up shouting, 'Everyone out of the pool, please.'

Roger and Mandy looked puzzled but got out and returned to their spot in the sun.

'What on earth is going on Roger?'

'I've no idea. Look, they're cordoning the whole pool off with red tape marked "Biological Danger". This is weird.'

Just then, a man emerged from the main building wearing a HazMat suit. He went over to the pool, jumped in and disappeared under the surface. About twenty seconds later, he resurfaced holding something short and brown in his hand. He climbed out of the pool and held it triumphantly above his head. 'OK folks, panic over,' he shouted, 'it's only a Mars bar.'

Roger and Mandy lay in the sun until it began to sink lower in the sky. 'Shall we go back to the hotel?' asked Roger. Mandy nodded.

They left the pool and walked back to the hotel. The others had already returned and were sitting in the lounge. George had a lot of photos spread out on a table in front of him and one large picture set in a frame for the wall of the club.

CHAPTER FORTY-ONE

The six left the hotel after an early breakfast and climbed into two taxis to take them back to the airport. George and Roger left the others in the departure lounge while they went to file their flight plan and get a Met report.

Up in the Met Office, they received a personal Met briefing by the RAF duty forecaster, who kept twiddling with his handlebar moustache. 'Now sit down you chaps and pay attention,' he said, tapping a chart with what looked like a broken billiard cue, 'I must say you've picked a wizard day to return, nothing but sunshine between here and Blighty.'

They then filed their flight plan with a very courteous RAF operations man.

'Damned nice of you civvie chaps to pay us a visit, what!' he said and then arranged a trip around the radar control room and a departure brief, both given by a pretty WRAF controller.

'It's a different world, isn't it?' said George as they went back down the stairs to collect the others from the departure lounge.

They took off and climbed to ten thousand feet for their flight back to Biarritz. It was uneventful, and George and Roger spent the time counting bullrings to alleviate the boredom.

They landed at Biarritz and climbed out of the aircraft to stretch their legs. A bowser drew up beside the aircraft and the driver stuck his head out of the window.

'Do you require fuel, Monsieur?'

'Yes please.'

'It's the same fuel man, surely he must remember us.'

'Let's hope not, we need to pull the same trick again.'

'That will be nine hundred francs, Monsieur,' said the fuel man, when he had filled the tanks.

George took out his wallet and handed him ninety pounds.

The fuel man frowned and pointed to the notice on the bowser.

George shrugged his shoulders and pointed to the money.

At this point, a look of realisation came over the fuel man's face, and he realised he had been caught again. He started waving his arms and swearing profusely at George. The noise attracted the attention of a French customs official, who having recognised them, performed a quick headcount and waved them all on their way.

They all got back in the aircraft but when George tried to start the engine, the propeller wouldn't turn, accompanied by a whine of a motor spinning.

'I think the Bendix is stuck,' said George. He tried again but got the same result. 'It needs a good thump.'

They got out of the aircraft and George started to remove the engine cowling. 'Roger, you go and find a big hammer and an iron bar. Try that maintenance hangar over there.'

George continued to remove the cowling while Roger shot off into the hangar. After a few minutes, Roger returned with the required items. George took them, placed one end of the iron bar on the starter motor and proceeded to give the other end a few hefty thumps with the hammer.

'OK Roger, before we replace the cowling, jump in and see if it engages.'

Roger got in and turned the key. Straight away the propeller began to turn, so Roger let the key go before the engine started. He jumped out and helped George replace the cowling. He picked up the tools and returned them to the hangar. They all got back into the aircraft and this time the engine started.

They took off and flew north up the French coast. The only notable thing on the return to Linton was there was some sea fog in the English Channel and both Jersey and Guernsey were a different shape, due to the fog covering various corners of the islands.

CHAPTER FORTY-TWO

They all walked back into the flying club bar after a brief visit to Customs.

'I could murder a pint and a peppered steak,' said George, 'I do hope Kingsley is back.' He shot a glance behind the bar and his eyes fell on a tall, thin man who was serving a customer with a beer. He was wearing a flowery shirt, Hareem pants and red shoes.

'What the f..'

'Oh hello George,' said Piers, emerging from the cellar, 'how did the trip go?'

'Fine thanks Piers,' replied George, not taking his eyes off Mr Hareem Pants, 'who the hell is that?'

'Oh, that's Daniel that I told you about. He's here to help until the boys are back.'

Piers looked around the group and spotted Guy.

'Ah, Guy. I've got some very bad news. All your disco gear has been stolen.'

'Brilliant!' said Mandy, 'now what was the very bad news? Has someone returned it?'

'Ha bloody ha,' said Guy, 'have you reported it to the police?'

'Yes, I noticed the broken window this morning. The police were here earlier. They're on the case.'

'Who would do such a thing?'

'Well a hundred musically discerning club members are probably helping the police with their enquiries as we speak, plus their guests, plus anyone else who has ever heard you, I should think,' said Mandy.

'Eight thousand Linton residents could be next in the frame,' said Roger.

'Kick a man when he's down, why don't you?' growled Guy and went off into the other room to see if anything was left.

'Now what would you all like to drink?' asked Piers.

'Five pints and a G and T at a guess, but first I'm starving. Can you get Dan started on a peppered steak please?'

Piers began pouring the drinks, while

Dan skipped off to the kitchen, his Hareem pants flapping.

'The boy's very light on his feet.'

'Isn't he just,' agreed Piers, admiringly.

'Now let's put the picture of the aircraft sitting in front of the Rock, upon the wall.'

George went over to the wall in the corner where they generally sat, pressed a self-adhesive hook onto the wall, and hung the picture.

'There, evidence of a successful trip.'

'Better make room for another picture, Alan and I are off to Gibraltar tomorrow.'

George turned around and Steve was standing there with a smirk on his face.

'So I hear, pity you're taking an instructor with you rather than going it alone though.'

The smirk on Steve's face changed to a look of anger. 'How do you know that?'

'Just an educated guess, you wouldn't make it without one on board.'

'You bastard.' Steve turned on his heel and walked out of the club.

Roger and Mandy finished their drinks. 'Well, we'll be off now. See you all soon I hope.'

They left the club and went into the car park. Roger had parked in the dark corner and took the opportunity to grope Mandy as they reached the car.

'Down boy, we've got all night for that in a comfortable bed.'

They got into the car and drove to Roger's house. When they arrived, they found the outside gate shut across the driveway and two cars parked on the drive.

'Alison!' hissed Roger.

'And Dan,' said Mandy, 'that's his car.'

'They must have broken in while we were away.'

'What do we do now, Roger?'

Roger thought for a moment. 'I don't think there's anything we can do tonight. I'll go and see my solicitor tomorrow morning. Let's drive back to the airport and get a room at the airport hotel.'

CHAPTER FORTY-THREE

It was nearly Christmas and Roger and Mandy were enjoying breakfast at the airport hotel. Several days had passed and Alison was resisting all attempts to get her out of the house, despite the best efforts of Roger's solicitor. Steve and Alan had returned from their Gibraltar trip and placed an identical picture on the club wall.

'What's your next move with Alison?' asked Mandy.

'I don't think I have one,' replied Roger, 'she's ignoring all solicitor's letters. I can't throw her out as she's in our matrimonial home.'

'Presumably, if you moved back in, she couldn't stop you being in the house, any more than you can stop her.'

'True, and I could kick Dan out, but think of the rows we would have. And what would happen to you? You'd have to go back to Dan. No. I won't do it. We are happy here together, and we would all be unhappy if I did, it's just not worth the hassle.'

'Well we can't stay here forever, this place must be costing you a fortune.'

'Well don't worry about that, I've got plans.'

'What are they, Roger?'

'I'll tell you when I've got something more concrete.'

'Well, I need to go to work. What are you doing today?'

'I'm going into London to collect my pilot's licence and to sort a few things out. I rang the CAA yesterday and told them not to put it in the post. If Alison gets her hands on it, she'll probably throw it on the fire. I'll see you in the club later on.'

CHAPTER FORTY-FOUR

Roger walked into the club bar. Mandy was already there, with George and Guy.

Mandy looked relieved, 'Roger, you're very late. I was getting worried.'

Roger, waved his new pilot's licence in the air, 'Look, I've got it!'

'Well done,' said George.

'I think drinks all round are in order,' said Roger, 'Daniel, can you arrange that please?'

Daniel came over and started pouring. George stuck his head over the bar. Daniel was wearing a tatty old pair of jeans, with split knees and frayed bottoms.

'No Hareem pants today then.'

'They're in the wash. So I'm wearing my new jeans today.'

George shook his head. 'I expect you paid

a lot for those. Do you know over the years, I've thrown hundreds of pairs of jeans away when they looked like that? If I had saved them, I could have bought an aircraft with the money I'd have made selling them to fools like you. It's ridiculous.'

'Talking of buying aircraft, how's it coming along?' asked Roger.

'Well, Steve talked Alan out of joining our group but the others are still on board. I suppose you've seen the picture of Alan's aircraft in front of the Rock?'

Roger looked over at the picture. 'Yes, I spotted it yesterday. Golf-Lima-Sierra-Tango-Golf. Looks like a nice aircraft.' He stopped and thought. 'I suppose the registration could also stand for Greg Led Steve To Gibraltar.'

'Oh, that's wonderful.' George got some Post-it notes out of his pocket. He took out his Biro and wrote Greg Led Steve To Gibraltar on one. He stuck the note on the picture. 'That will upset Steve!'

Malcolm walked over from the other end of the bar. 'Hello, Roger. Was that your new pilot's licence you were waving as you came in?'

'Yes. I got it today.'

'Congratulations. Linton Flying Club is doing quite well at the moment, with two trips to Gibraltar in the last week and two lovely pictures on the wall of the club. But at least your trip didn't get lost.'

'You mean the other one did?' asked George, his ears pricking up.

'Yes. I heard from a French controller, who got the info from a Spanish controller. No more details I'm afraid.'

'Well, thanks for the heads up.'

'No problem. Well, I must be off. Well done on the licence, Roger.'

'Thanks, Malcolm.'

'What a bit of info that was. They actually got lost!'

Roger looked across at the picture. 'I think I feel another one coming George. How about Get Lost Steve Told Greg.'

When George had stopped laughing, he got out another Post-it note and wrote Get Lost Steve Told Greg, so he did! He went over and stuck it to the picture. 'This just gets better and better!'

CHAPTER FORTY-FIVE

'It's peppered steak time, I think,' said George, 'Piers, can you oblige please?'

'Daniel, peppered steak for George, please. Now I hope you will all be here on Christmas Eve as the boys will be back and Fidel always does something special on Christmas and New Years Eve.'

'What exactly?' asked Mandy.

'Well, he does a drag act, dresses outrageously. And if the replacement disco gear arrives in time, Guy will be doing a Christmas Eve disco. I expect people will dress up for the occasion.'

'Sounded quite good up to that point but I suppose we will be here, won't we Roger?'

'Yes, where else would we be.'

'I took Fidel into town last week to buy

his new outfit,' said Guy.

'Took him to your personal dressmaker did you?' asked Mandy.

Guy stuck his tongue out at her.

'Now George, you keep getting bigger and bigger,' said Roger, 'Your missus hasn't got you pregnant, has she?'

'Cheeky git,' said George, 'Yes, I suppose I've put on a bit of weight.'

'Is she fattening you up like a goose for Christmas?'

'No. My mate Len always gives me a goose for Christmas.'

'Well, your sex life is your own, George. No one will judge.'

'Not that sort of goose, you idiot.'

'So why all the weight?'

'Well I leave home at five-thirty in the morning to drive into London, so I always stop off at a Cafe on the way and eat a double fry up. Come lunchtime, there is always one of the brown-nosing contractors who will take me out to lunch, so a nice meal and a bottle of wine. When I get home at night, the missus has made me some dinner and then I come up here and eat a nice peppered steak. But I think it must be the biscuits I eat before I go to bed that's causing it.'

'There is an amazing amount of calories in what you eat George,' said Mandy, 'and I don't suppose you do much exercise, do you?'

'No, the missus has gone off that a bit recently.'

'I bet you haven't seen your cock in a long time either,' said Guy, 'I think you might have an overactive err um..'

'Thyroid gland?' suggested Mandy.

'No, knife and fork,' continued Guy.

'Oh look out,' said Roger, 'here comes Steve.'

Steve came into the bar. He looked over at his picture and noticed the Post-it notes stuck to it. He went over, read them, ripped them off and came straight over to George.

'What do you think you are doing? Sticking this crap on my picture.'

'Just a joke. I think you're having a sense of humour failure.'

'I don't see anything funny in these.'

'Well you had to take Greg with you to get you to Gibraltar and even he got lost, didn't he.'

'How the hell did you know that?'

'Because I've got spies everywhere.'

Steve stood for a few seconds, his mouth moving but with no sound coming out. He finally managed to summon up some words. 'You'll regret this George.' He threw the Post-it notes on the floor, turned on his heel and left.

'George, your peppered steak is ready,' shouted Daniel.

George went to the bar, picked up his food and went off looking for a place to sit down.

Soon Roger heard the unmistakable squawk of Seymour as Captain Slack's crew came through the door of the bar.

'Oh look Kyle, it's your Dilly boy again. He can't keep away. I'm sure he's got a hard spot for you.'

'I can assure you I haven't,' said Roger with a laugh.

They were followed in by the rest of the crew. Sandy glanced at Roger as she walked in, then saw he was with Mandy and went straight to the other end of the bar. Beverley spotted Guy and quickly joined her.

'So are you people all ready for Christmas?' asked Kyle.

'I'm not,' said Guy, 'I just rang Alcohol Concern. I told them I was worried I didn't have enough beer in the fridge to last until Boxing Day. They can be quite rude, can't they?'

CHAPTER FORTY-SIX

Christmas Eve arrived and the Flying School remained closed. Mandy went into town to buy a new dress for the Christmas Eve disco and Roger was rather mysterious, spending quite a while on the phone. When Mandy asked him what he was up to, he replied that he was making plans but yet again, he refused to elaborate. Guy took delivery of some new disco gear and spent the day putting the parts together only to find there were no speakers.

In their hotel room, Roger and Mandy were getting ready. Mandy struggled to put her new dress on, and once inside, found parts of her wanted to pop back outside.

'You don't think this dress is too low cut, do you Roger?'

Roger turned round. 'OK, just lean forward a bit. That's fine. Now tell me, have you got a hairy chest?'

'Of course not.'

'In that case, it's definitely too low cut.'

'Don't mess about Roger. Does it look alright?'

'It looks fine. Doesn't leave much to the imagination though. I'm sure you'll be turning a few heads and tightening a few pairs of trousers.'

'OK, well I'm ready when you are.'

'I'm ready. Shall we walk?'

They walked up the road to the club. The bar was heaving, and they had to push their way across to reach the end where George, Guy, Enis and Charlie were all standing.

'Enis,' said Mandy, 'so nice to see you again. How is the tattoo parlour doing?'

'Very well Mandy. Nice to see you and Roger as well. Sorry, I haven't been around but parlour is so busy that I don't usually get up here until late.'

'Wow, never seen the club this full,' said Mandy.

'Did your disco gear arrive OK, Guy?' asked Roger.

'Yes but minus any speakers.'

'Oh that accounts for the full house,' said Mandy, 'word's got around.'

'Ha-bloody-ha. Daniel's gone home to get his. He should be back shortly.'

'Well let's make the most of it until then,' said Mandy.

'I must say you look absolutely gorgeous tonight Mandy,' said Guy, 'do you mind if I touch your hair?'

Mandy looked surprised. 'If you must.'

Guy ran his finger along Mandy's top lip.

Mandy gasped. She threw a punch at Guy but missed.

'Steady on people, remember it's Christmas,' said George.

Mandy scowled at Guy. She turned to Roger. 'Roger, I'm gasping for a G and T.'

Roger bought a round of drinks. 'Cheers everybody. Merry Christmas to you all. So what are you all doing tomorrow? Turkey dinner followed by the Queen's Speech followed by playing Charades?'

'No, I won't be playing Charades anymore,' said Guy, 'I had an unfortunate experience playing Charades.'

'Why doesn't that surprise me, Guy,' said Mandy, 'OK, what happened?'

'Well, when my turn came, I picked a pop

song out of the hat, "Come On Eileen". Now unfortunately, Eileen just wouldn't see the funny side of it. She called me a filthy git and said I'd ruined her brand-new cashmere jumper. It cost me nearly a hundred pounds to replace it. Never again!'

They all looked at Guy in stunned silence.

George recovered first. 'Has anybody got an advent calendar? I've got the Jehovah's Witness advent calendar this year. It's so realistic. Every time you open one of the doors, a voice says 'Oh do fuck off!'

They all laughed.

'Well at least Advent calendars bring some religious side into Christmas,' said Charlie, 'Christmas is supposed to be a religious festival celebrating the birth of a special baby, but the only time most people mention Jesus Christ at Christmas nowadays is when they see the price of presents!'

They all laughed again.

'When I was with Alison, I felt I was turning in to Father Christmas,' said Roger.

They all looked at him, puzzled.

'Well, Father Christmas only comes once a year.'

They all laughed again.

'Mind you, he comes down the chimney. I've never done that.'

They all laughed again.

'This is turning into a joke session,' said Charlie, 'remember what happened in Gibraltar Guy, the womenfolk left us.'

'And you got a slap round the face,' laughed Guy.

'Perhaps we should cool it a bit, in case someone goes overboard with a joke and the same happens.'

Just then Daniel walked through the door carrying a large speaker cabinet.

'Brilliant,' shouted Guy and ran off with Enis to give him a hand.

Roger looked around the bar. His eyes rested on the far wall where their picture of Gibraltar should be. It was empty.

'George, our Gibraltar picture has disappeared.'

George spun round. 'You're right, it's gone. Well, no prizes for guessing who took that. He said I'd regret it.'

CHAPTER FORTY-SEVEN

Suddenly, Guy started his disco.

'Hello and welcome to the Christmas Eve Cloud Nine Disco with your host Prince Charles. Well hasn't the weather been awful? It's been raining longer than my bloody mother. I had to take an umbrella with me the other day when I opened a book shop in London. The nice young lady that owned it asked me if I liked Dickens. I had to tell her I had no idea, I've never been invited to one. And as I came out tonight, I left Diana watching the TV. She said I see butter's going up again. I said what are you watching my dear, the shopping channel? She said no, Last Tango in Paris. So let's start tonight on a French theme with Je t'aime moi non plus by Serge Gainsbourg

194

and Jane Birkin.'

Je t'aime moi non plus started playing in the background.

Roger turned to George. 'I'm afraid I'm going to drop out of buying into the aircraft George.'

'Why on earth is that?' asked George, 'I thought you were really keen.'

'I was, but I can't stand these continual problems with Alison. I know now what I want to do in life, and it's flying. I've been talking to flying schools in Florida and I've decided to go to the USA to continue my flight training. The weather is always nice and the price of training is a fraction of what it costs here. So I leave on Boxing Day.'

Nobody saw Mandy slip quietly away with tears in her eyes.

'I wish you the best of luck, Roger,' said George, 'I presume you've checked out whether they will let you into the USA or not. They can be very funny over there. I mean, have you got a criminal record?'

'Well, I actually possess an LP of Max Bygraves singing Christmas carols. Would that count?'

George laughed. 'OK, I guess you checked it all out. Don't worry about the

195

aircraft, I think we've got enough people to get the project off the ground. Maybe you might like to buy in when you come back.'

'Quite probably. I shall be back for my divorce from Alison. I'm leaving it all in my solicitor's hands, so I can concentrate on my flying and on Mandy,' he looked round, 'where is she?'

'I don't know, she was right next to you.'

'I was just plucking up the courage to ask her to come with me.'

Enis came running up. 'Roger, what is wrong with Mandy? She in tears as she passed in lobby and ran into toilet.'

Roger looked puzzled. He turned to George. 'You don't suppose she heard me tell you about the USA and assumed I was leaving her behind?'

'She may well have done.'

'Enis, the toilet you said?'

'Yes.'

Roger shot out of the door into the lobby. He hesitated before running into the Ladies, and gingerly opened the door. Luckily, there was no one visible but one closet door was closed. Roger listened carefully and he could hear sobbing. He walked over to the door and knocked. 'Mandy? Mandy?

What's the matter? Why are you crying?'

'Go away Roger. Go to the USA. Go and leave me with nothing, if your flying means that much to you. I knew you were up to something when you wouldn't explain all those phone calls.'

'Mandy, if you had waited another ten seconds, I would have asked you, no, I would have implored you, to come with me. How could you think I would leave you here?'

The sobbing abated. 'Roger, do you mean that? You want me to come with you?'

'Of course, I do Mandy. Why else would I have bought two first-class tickets to Florida? We leave the day after tomorrow on Boxing Day. I was so worried you wouldn't want to come with me.'

The bolt on the closet slid back, the door opened and Mandy appeared. She threw her arms around Roger. 'Of course, I want to come with you. I've nothing left here.'

'That's settled then. I thought, with your experience of flying clubs, it should be easy for you to get a job in reception, like here. I haven't finally decided which club to go with, I thought we'd look at a few and see which one we liked the best.'

'Oh yes, one that has a bar, a resident DJ, and a bunch of wonderful people like we have at the Linton Flying Club.'

They walked hand-in-hand back into the bar just as Guy put some music on and announced that Fidel was starting his drag act.

Fidel appeared in a black PVC mini-dress, with matching black PVC knickers, stockings and suspenders, a long black wig, a large pair of wobbly false breasts, and he carried a whip. He cavorted around the room, using the whip to pull men towards him and pretending to kiss them. When he reached Kyle and Seymour there was no need for pretence as they both embraced him and started to snog him. They danced around the room in a threesome to the shouts from the crowd.

When the music ended, Fidel went to the stage and proceeded to sing "Hey Big Spender". He finished to a standing ovation from the crowd.

Roger turned to Mandy and gave her a kiss. 'I doubt we'll ever find a club anywhere in the world to match The Linton Flying Club!'

Printed in Great Britain
by Amazon

65138636R00119